W9-CBG-257

See you later, Crocodile

Also by Georgess McHargue

THE BEASTS OF NEVER
THE TALKING TABLE MYSTERY
THE TURQUOISE TOAD MYSTERY
FUNNY BANANAS
THE IMPOSSIBLE PEOPLE
THE HORSEMAN'S WORD
STONEFLIGHT

See you later, Crocodile

Georgess McHargue

Published by
Delacorte Press
The Bantam Doubleday Dell Publishing Group, Inc.
666 Fifth Avenue
New York, New York 10103

Library of Congress Cataloging in Publication Data
McHargue, Georgess.
See you later, crocodile / by Georgess McHargue.
p. cm.
Summary: When she inadvertently befriends eccentric Aunt Aggie, who keeps cats and is passionate about their welfare, shy, thirteen-year-old Johanna learns a great deal about the difficulties of old age and of maintaining a friendship with a stubborn and opinionated old lady.
ISBN 0-440-50052-4
[1. Old age—Fiction. 2. Friendship—Fiction. 3. Cats—Fiction.]
I. Title.
PZ7.M183Se 1988
[Fic]—dc19 88-6504
CIP
AC

Manufactured in the United States of America

September 1988

10 9 8 7 6 5 4 3 2 1

BG

To Mairi, who was there.
And to the memory of Gertrude Foss, 1895–1982

The author would also like to thank the MacDowell Colony of Peterborough, New Hampshire, where the first draft of this book was written.

CHAPTER 1

WHEN I answered the phone in the upstairs hall that night, I almost didn't recognize the voice, it was so thin and thready. "That you, Joan?" it asked. The time was after midnight, the cold carpet was gritty under my toes, and I had thought it would be my mom, saying they'd be home late from the Concord Band concert.

"Mrs. Pease?" I said. "Is that you?"

"I need some help," she said. "Cahn't seem to get myself up. C'n you come ovuh?"

"Mrs. Pease! What's the matter? Did you fall?"

"Yes, I fell!" She sounded resentful now. "Just caught m'foot on some newspaypuhs. Now come along like a good gel and help me up. You know wheyuh the keys ah."

By now I was completely awake and trying to think fast. I understood why Mrs. Pease had called me, even though I was just a kid: I was close. In daylight I could cut through backyards and be at her house in two minutes. And there were reasons why nobody who lived closer was likely to help her—not quickly, not at night, and maybe not ever. "I'll be there," I said. "Mrs. Pease, I'll be right there. But you have to call somebody else, too. Mrs. Parker, maybe." A grown-up was what I meant.

Mrs. Pease gave a *hmph,* sounding quite like herself. "I done that a'ready, but she wan't get here a while. Youa big enough to do what I want. Now don't stand theyuh gabbin'." She hung up, and that was just like her too.

I threw on jeans and a sweater, scrawled a note for my parents, and ran.

By the time I got to Mrs. Pease's house on Oak Street, it seemed unreal to be running around in the middle of the night. Everything was quiet under the streetlights, and even the bare wisteria vine writhing over the porch looked just as it always did. I didn't like the idea of putting my fingers in the damp, musty seeds and bird droppings in the bird feeder where the spare keys were, but I did it and managed the two locks. Over the shrill barking of Annie the dog I could hear Mrs. Pease's voice faintly from my left.

"It's all right, Mrs. Pease, it's me, Jo," I called. "I know where you are."

I had never been in "the animal room" before. Usually when Boots and I came, it was in the afternoon, and we sat out on the front porch or in the parlor to the right, crowded with cut glass and old valentines. I knew the way, though. Cats were already rubbing and stretching at the screen door beyond the staircase. I unlatched it, trying not to trip on cats, turned left in the kitchen and left again into the front room, the animal room.

It was a shock to see her there on the floor, with her thin, blue-veined legs spread wide in front of her, and her torn pink nightdress halfway up her thighs. She was leaning on a little table that looked as if it would fall over any minute, and the old black telephone was between her knees. I knelt beside her, and she reached out and took my wrist. "Help me get up, Joan," she said. "I cahn't seem to get up."

"Where does it hurt?" I asked.

"I ain't *huht,* just shocked. Wouldn't I know if I was huht? Now just get me up, I want to get back to bed. It's drafty down heyuh."

As a matter of fact, the room was as warm as an August day because of the huge old coal stove in the kitchen. I looked at Mrs. Pease again, and saw that her left leg was turned way out so the outside of her foot was almost flat on the floor.

"Mrs. Pease, I can't get you up. I think I ought to call a doctor."

Her face went into a scowl. "No doctuh, you hea me?"

She shivered, and I pulled a blanket off the bed and put it around her. "Can you move your left foot?" I asked.

"Why should I want to do that?" But I could see from her mouth and the cords in her neck that she had made an effort, though the foot stayed where it was.

"I'm calling for help," I said, and before she could begin to argue, I reached for the phone. She had been right about one thing: I could easily have lifted her, though I'm only in the eighth grade. She looked like an old-fashioned doll sprawled on the floor—the kind with china arms and legs and head. I was strong enough, but I wasn't feeling old enough, and I wanted somebody else, fast.

On the side of the phone was a grubby piece of adhesive tape with *Dr. Finnegan* and a number written on it, but I knew the name was her vet's, not her doctor's. I called the emergency number 911 and said what I had to say. Then I hung up and went back to Mrs. Pease. "No doctuh," she was saying. "I don't want no doctuh. They ruined my foot and they ruined my hip, that time, and that Mrs. Langley, she took all my things."

"Mrs. Pease," I said, trying to sound the way I do when I have to tell Boots there isn't any more candy, "if I pull you up and something is broken, I could make it a lot worse, don't you see? Then if you do go to the hospital, you'd have to stay

longer." I had reached out and taken her hand, and suddenly she was holding on and crying a little.

"But my babies? Who'll take cayuh of my babies?" she asked. A noise made me turn around, and there was a tall, weathered man in an orange parka with an emergency medical technician's patch on the sleeve. I was relieved to see it was not a stranger but Mr. Carson, whose daughter Jenny is in my class. He had two other EMTs with him, and through the front window I could see the flashing lights of the ambulance.

They got right to work on Mrs. Pease. To get out of the way, I went and sat on a rocking chair, while the brown tabby kitten, Cuddles, climbed up my sweater and played with the ends of my hair.

The ambulance people were wonderful. They knew exactly what to do and they didn't seem surprised at Mrs. Pease's bedroom—the animal room. I, on the other hand, couldn't keep from looking around at it. I knew I had never imagined what it was really like. The linoleum on the floor wasn't tacked down but lay in sheets with curled-up edges. Newspapers were scattered over it, with cat footprints, spots of cat food, and a couple of cat messes on them. The bed was just a daybed, without head or foot, and the sheets and blankets were so old and gray, they looked as if they were woven out of cat hair. The only light in the room was from a bare bulb in a wall fixture, and where it shone along the walls you could see that the tan-and-maroon wallpaper was hanging in strips, and cobwebs were draped like fishnets in the corners of the ceiling. By the bed were a little brown plastic radio and the cigar box full of odds and ends that Mrs. Pease always kept with her. The only other pieces of furniture were the rocker I was sitting in, another one draped in old clothes, a dark wooden bureau with three knobs missing, and a little old trunk with wooden bands across the top. At any one time there were at least eight cats in the room. Right now Midnight, Whitey, Goldie, Dolly, Fiddle, and Mummy were lying on the furniture, the mantel, or the floor, Cuddles and the little tortoiseshell called Pooky were playing with a spoon on the bed, and Lavender, the young Siamese, was parading around the edges of the room yowling like a ghost in a graveyard. Mrs. Pease had a million cats, and everything was covered with a thin skin of cat hair and dust. The only thing that looked at all new was a shiny black-and-silver police monitor on the windowsill by the bed. It began to sputter and crackle. "Accident on Oak Street, Charlie. It's Mrs. Pease. Better get on over." *No wonder she always knows what's going on before it's in the paper,* I thought.

At this point the EMTs started bringing in a stretcher. Mrs. Pease said she didn't want to get on it, but one of them, a young woman with a blond ponytail, sat down by her on the floor and talked to her, and pretty soon they were able to slide her over onto it. Then the policeman arrived and beckoned me into the kitchen. He was short, with a stiff brown mustache and friendly brown eyes. He introduced himself as Officer Savineau. How did I come to be there? he wanted to know, and who was Mrs. Pease's closest relative?

"She doesn't have any," I explained. "She had a sister, but they weren't speaking, and anyway, she died." No children? Nieces? Nephews? I told him no.

While we were talking, the EMTs had got Mrs. Pease out the door on the stretcher. "My kitties!" she was calling. "Don't let them out." Somehow, the policeman and I and one of the EMTs got all the cats back in the kitchen, except for Goldie, who ran upstairs as usual. I decided I could get him later.

They put Mrs. Pease in the ambulance, and at that moment Mrs. Parker arrived. She was a small, tight, energetic person with ginger hair, who seemed to know all the EMTs. I had only met her once before, but I knew she "did things" for Mrs. Pease. Now I found out that she worked at the hospital. She told Mr. Carson she'd follow the ambulance.

"Where's her purse, Jo?" she asked me. "We'll need her Medicare number and so on." I went back in and got the purse from where I had seen it tucked down beside the daybed, half hidden in the sheets and blankets. It was a long, hard thing made of red plastic, with a scratched brass clasp at the top. Mrs. Parker got something out and pressed it into my hand. "Her keys," she said. "She wants you to have her keys." Then she looked up at me and grinned. *"How'd you do it, kiddo?* There aren't six people in this town that could have made Aggie Pease call a doctor. That hip is broken, you know. Now, you lock up the house and Charlie Savineau is going to drive you home. It's late." She got in her own car and followed the big white box as it pulled away from the curb.

I looked at the keys in my hand. "Well, Miss Morse," said Officer Savineau, "looks like you've inherited quite a family." We went inside, hauled Goldie out from under the hat stand in the upstairs hall, made sure all the windows were shut, and stood looking doubtfully at the kitchen stove.

"Should we do anything to that?" I asked. "Maybe it needs more coal or something."

"Beats me," he said. "I haven't seen a monster like that since my great-grandpa died. I guess we'd best leave it alone."

As we pulled up in front of my house, Dad and Mother were just going in the door. "Now, folks, don't get all upset," said Officer Savineau, as if the sight of me coming home in a police car might have made them throw me out of the house forever. Dad gave me a hug and then pulled back.

"You don't have to tell me where you've been," he said. "I can smell cats. What happened?"

I realized I had hardly noticed the smell this time, I was so used to it. "I'll tell you all about it," I promised, "just as soon as I take a shower."

CHAPTER 2

I had met Mrs. Pease one October day when Boots and I were out looking for my cat, Watermelon. Ordinarily, Watermelon thinks he is too grand to honor the outdoors with his presence, and just lies around the house purring and looking magnificent, which is fine with us because he isn't at all bright about cars and Deming is a busy street. However, this was one of those tricky days we get in Massachusetts when they're trying to fool you into believing there won't be any winter, and I guess even a twenty-four-pound cat can't resist all that blue and gold, when every rustle in the leaves might be a nice fat chipmunk. The town of Vicinity is very good at fall, and busloads of people from Boston come through on October weekends just as if our trees could do a clever trick the ones on Boston Common didn't know.

Boots was scuffing up the leaves with his cowboy boots, the ones he's named for because his real name is Bateman Lister, III, and nobody who's three can be called Bateman. The beech leaves were just the color of his hair. It's hard not to forget whatever else you're doing when you look at Boots, because he not only has that mop of silky gold hair, but huge blue eyes and a turned-up nose with exactly six freckles and a three-cornered smile that makes grown-ups let him get away with absolute mayhem. Every third kick, he was calling out, "Watermeow! Watermeow!" which is what he always calls Watermelon. We were halfway down the block between Main Street and Concord, when a hoarse, high voice said, "That yuh little brothuh?"

"He's not my brother," I said politely. "I baby-sit for him in the afternoons. His name is Boots." I knew it was Mrs. Pease, of course, because everybody knew her house, the one with no paint and no lawn, just weeds and a big snaky wisteria vine all over the little front porch. I didn't come by there very often, but I knew that people used to tighten the corners of their mouths and say, "Isn't that a shame?" whenever Mrs. Pease, or Mrs. Pease's house, or even Oak Street, was mentioned. I didn't find out until later what "Isn't that a shame?" really meant.

At first, standing out there in the bright sun, I

couldn't see anyone, and then I saw her sitting in a folding chair in the shadow of the wisteria, looking as bare and gray as the wood on the porch. She was still watching Boots, who had stopped kicking and calling and was trying to climb up on her little rough stone gatepost. The gate was gone but there were rusty iron brackets shaped like beckoning fingers where it must have hung.

"Ain't he cunnin'?" said Mrs. Pease to me. "Now, you come up heyuh, young man. Aggie has somethin' fuh yuh." There was a cigar box on the porch floor beside her. She fumbled in it a minute and then pulled out a little heart-shaped tin, the kind with fruit drops in it. The thought came to me that she was the witch with the candy house and funny little Boots was Hansel, but the next minute I was ashamed of myself. Besides, it was far too late to stop Boots, who had clattered up the steps to the porch and was choosing a fruit drop as carefully as if it had been a magic wish offered by the Blue Fairy. I followed him up, half thinking I would get one, too, but after Boots had settled on red, Mrs. Pease snapped the box shut and said to me, "You missin' a cat?" I was so surprised that I stared at her. Up close, she was mostly nose and bones, inside a housedress with a zippered front and an all-over pattern of pinkish-grayish flowers. The skin of her legs was mottled with blue and red, and there were torn terry-cloth slippers on her feet, held on with rubber bands.

"How did you know about my cat?" I asked, and I sat down on the porch step without being asked because lately there is so much of my legs that they want to fold up whenever anybody may be looking at them.

She made a *hmph* in her throat and gestured behind her with her head. "Don't you think I got eyes?" she asked. "Fust a big old cat with stripes like a melon comes inta my yahd—been out talkin' to my babies all the forenoon. Then you come along, the two of yuh, callin' out a name for a cat with stripes. No, I ain't blind yet, nor silly neithuh." She put out a hand to stop me as I began to get up. "Don't go aftuh him just yet. You cahn't get in that gate till I open it from inside. But he's thayuh, all right. Socializin'." Suddenly she shut her knobby hand around my wrist and her eyes got fierce. "What you mean lettin' that nice big kitty out, anyway? Don't you know he could get stole, or run ovuh?"

Her hand felt hard and surprisingly strong, but I liked her suddenly for caring about Watermelon. "We *don't* let him out," I explained. "Usually he doesn't even like to go out. I guess it's the nice weather. Are you sure he's in your backyard? He's a very big, long-haired tiger with just a white splash on his chin and one white hind foot. Really, I think I'd better get him now before he goes off somewhere else. He's all mine and we're very attached to each other."

Mrs. Pease let me go and began pushing down on the aluminum arms of her chair. I saw she was struggling to get up, and put out a hand to help her. It took quite a heave to get her out of the chair, and I forgot I was standing on the steps and almost fell over backward. I was glad when she didn't seem to notice. She picked up a broom that was propped against the house door and leaned on it as she worked her way to where she could pull the door toward her. The broom was so old that it was almost bald. What was left of its straws made a crunchy noise each time she leaned on it. I thought about witches again, but it was clear no flying was going on here.

Boots was watching Mrs. Pease with big round eyes. I doubt if he had ever met anyone that old before; I wasn't sure I had myself. "Don't worry," she said to me. "I can manage. You go 'round to the side gate, and I'll let you in to meet my babies." The thick, battered green door shut behind her and Boots and I were alone on the porch.

"Come on, Cowboy," I said to him, "let's go see where Watermelon is." We picked our way around the house, stepping over the plants in the tangled front garden. A lot were in pots sunk in the ground —things like azaleas and English ivy. In several places were the cinnamon-colored berries of false Solomon's seal, and at the house corner was a big bunch of royal purple New England asters, a favorite of my mother's. It was Mom, too, who'd taught me to recognize the little dark leaves of the patch of wintergreen growing in the shade around the corner from the porch. I'd never seen it in a garden before, only in the deep woods.

The gate was almost hidden by a big swag of bittersweet, all covered with clumps of orange berries cupped in little gold husks like baby's fingernails. The fence was much higher than my head, and so was the gate, though you could see through it a little bit in places where the boards had broken and chicken wire had been nailed over.

We waited. After several minutes, Boots announced, "I wanta go home." Even I was beginning to wonder if I really wanted to find out what lay behind that gate. If it had been anything but Watermelon, I think I might have left.

At last, there came a shuffling and a scraping, a chain rattled, and Mrs. Pease opened the gate. She had put on a baby-pink sweater with pearl buttons, and Watermelon was in her arms, hooking his big claws in and out of the sweater (it was raveled all over) and purring like an oil furnace. "The sweet, sweet boy!" she said. "He come right up to me, nice as you please." I was amazed that she could have lifted Watermelon, who, besides being heavy, goes all limp and ecstatic the minute you pick him up.

I started to unhook him from the sweater, but stared around the yard instead. At first it looked like a marionette theater. There were crisscrossed wires overhead with strings hanging down from them, and on the end of every string was a cat. There were big ones, little ones, gray ones, yellow ones, young ones, old ones, everywhere you looked: cats lying, cats standing, cats washing, cats sleeping, cats batting lazily at flies. Boots, who likes anything with fur, had already picked up a black cat by the middle.

"Be nice to the pussycat, Boots," I said. "He doesn't know you and he might scratch."

"Scratch?" Mrs. Pease sounded offended. "He's a good boy, my Niggy is. He won't scratch the child. What did you say his name is?"

"Boots," I said.

"Boots? That ain't a name for a Christian, that's a name for a cat. My Bootsie's gone now, sweet little thing. Now, you tell me that little boy's *baptismal* name."

I thought about Boots's mama and all of Boots's various "stepdaddies," at least the ones I'd heard about, and I doubted that Mrs. Vesey had ever gotten herself together enough to baptize Boots, even if she went in for baptism, but I said, "Cowboy, tell Mrs. Pease your real name."

Boots stood up straight, the way I knew he would, wrinkled his button nose, scrunched up his eyes, and recited, "My name is Bateman Lister *the* Third, and I live at fordy-three Pond Lane in Vicinity, Mastachuzitts, and I am three years old and I'm gonna be a *cowboy*." He opened his eyes and went back to patting the black cat, very fast, as if to make up for lost time.

"Well, ain't he the darlingest thing! He's a little angel child, that's what he is."

I was tired of Mrs. Pease's talking about Boots all the time and more or less ignoring me. I was wondering how I could leave politely, when she announced, "Well, I wun't keep you. It's time I fixed suppa fuh me and the babies. Heyuh, Bobby, have another little sweet from Aggie." She bent over Boots with the candy tin, and he took one solemnly, then put up his round, soft arms and kissed the thin, papery skin of her neck.

Mrs. Pease's mouth puckered into a surprised O, and two spots of bright pink came into her cheeks. I wondered how long it had been since anybody, anybody at all, had kissed her. Then I promised Boots in my mind an extralong swing session at the playground and thanked Mrs. Pease for the candy and for finding Watermelon. Just as we started down the drive, her voice came to me through the fence. "You! Gel! What you say yuh name was?"

"Johanna. I'm Jo Morse, Mrs. Pease. I live on Deming Street."

"Well, you come again, Joan, and bring that little angel Bobby. You come see Aggie and she'll give you somethin' real nice."

Even if I'd been planning to, I wouldn't have hurried back to Mrs. Pease's, because of what happened the next week. Ever since the previous spring, my parents had been trying to open a new kind of bookstore—one that sold used paperbacks at prices people could afford—but getting a bank loan took a long time and there had been moments, I knew, when they thought it would never come through.

"We're going to have to work like hell," Dad warned, the night the good news finally came, but he didn't sound worried, and I knew that it was *not working* that had made him depressed last summer. If running a bookstore that sold used paperbacks was going to make him cheerful again, I was all in favor of it.

CHAPTER 3

AFTER the excitement about the loan died down, I found I was seeing more of Boots and a lot less of my parents because they were busy making arrangements about the new bookstore. Sometimes I felt a little left out. Then I remembered that Boots had probably been feeling that way all his life.

I baby-sit for Boots in the afternoons because his mother is going to art school or something in Boston. Her name is Cynthia Vesey, and she has soft, shining blond hair just like Boots's, a dark blue Mercedes car, and a third or fourth husband who left her and went to Brazil. Her wristwatch has six diamonds on it, her fingernails are royal purple, and if she ever has to put on a Band-Aid, I'm sure it has a designer label. In Vicinity, she looks the way a blue and yellow and red jungle parrot would look if it landed on your bird feeder with the juncos and chickadees. It's not that nobody in Vicinity has money, it's that the richer you are around here, the more likely you are to wear jeans to town meeting and drive a Jeep with a snowplow on the front.

I was glad for Boots that he was nice to look at, because otherwise she probably would have sent him back to Neiman-Marcus for a refund. I mention Neiman-Marcus because it's a Texas store and I know Boots's real father has a ranch in Texas and once went to jail for trying to bribe a senator. Boots and his mother live in Vicinity because Cynthia inherited a house here and had nowhere else to go. Boots has lived in Fort Worth, Palm Springs, San Francisco, and Vicinity, each place with a different father or stepfather. I thought that must have something to do with the fact that my pal Boots didn't often try anything new but seemed to wait for things to happen to him. It was one reason why I'd been surprised and pleased when he took to Mrs. Pease, that day when we found Watermelon.

After a while Boots and I were going over to Mrs. Pease's a couple of times a week. Partly, it gave us something to do, now that snow was on the ground. Partly, I had discovered how hard it was for Mrs. Pease to do things with her hands. She was strong enough to carry the cats, open doors, and so on, but anything small and fussy she could hardly handle at all. "It's that dahned ahthuritis," she would say as she kept right on trying to pick up the scissors or open her change purse. It might take her two whole minutes to unbutton her sweater, and writing was even more complicated because her hands shook.

I began by writing her shopping lists for her once a week. A person named Lily apparently did her shopping, but Lily had trouble reading Mrs. Pease's writing. Now she got mine instead: *stew meat, canned peas, little cakes, turkey legs, canned carrots, cottage cheese, potatoes, Little Friskies, whole wheat bread, real butter, and grape juice,* those were the things on most of her shopping lists. She never bought margarine ("It gives you worms"), and I learned that she had her milk delivered from a special farm outside town that sold it "raw." The grape juice helped her arthritis, she said, but everything else she cooked was the same for herself as for the animals—meat and vegetables stewed together.

When I wasn't doing lists, I sometimes sewed things for her, though she didn't think much of the way I did it. "In my day, a gel had to sew a fine seam, *a fine seam,* or she'd nevuh get a husband." Still, I thought the drooping hems and torn sleeves I fixed for her looked better than they had before.

While I was sewing or opening her mail, Boots would be happily occupied with the rocking horse or one of the other things he had found to play with in Mrs. Pease's parlor. She was Aunt Aggie to him now, and "Thunder" was his favorite toy in the world. The big, old-fashioned rocking horse was about six inches taller than Boots and covered in brown horsehide, with a real horsehair mane and tail. His one remaining eye was brown glass and his brown wooden nose had big red nostrils. One skirt of his leather saddle was gone, but the reins were still on, and best of all, his rockers were long and strong, curved high at the ends.

Boots would rock happily on Thunder for half an hour at a time. Sometimes he got so absorbed, I thought he was nearly asleep with his eyes open, and I would have to lift him off by his soft round middle and get him to play with the little old wooden cow barn with the three painted cows or else the wonderful cast-iron bank shaped like an elephant, which tossed a penny into a slot on its back with its trunk whenever you pulled its tail. As time went on, I started bringing my own supply of pennies because Mrs. Pease would insist on giving Boots a handful to play with, and by then I knew she had hardly enough money for turkey legs.

The first time I saw a "Notice of Discontinuance" in her mail, it was from the gas company. The next time, it was the telephone, but she seemed to pay no attention. The rest of the mail consisted mostly of magazines and newsletters from the Friends of Animals, the Humane Society, and the ASPCA. Boots always liked to have her show him the pictures of the dogs and cats inside. He didn't understand why her animals weren't allowed to run all over so he could play with them, and the back part of the house, containing the kitchen, the "shed," and the animal room, was off limits behind its screen door. Mrs. Pease usually brought in just one favorite cat when we came, and that one most often was Mummy, a tabby so ancient that if Mrs. Pease was right about her age, she was over a hundred in human years.

That day, there was a picture of a Saint Bernard on a magazine cover that reminded her of something. "Would you like to see Aunt Aggie with a big doggie like that?" she asked Boots. Boots is as bad as I am about "speaking up" sometimes, but for different reasons. I learned long ago that if I say what's on my mind, some people don't like it. In Boots's case, he knows he's so adorable he doesn't have to bother. He just nodded.

Mrs. Pease picked up the wooden cigar box she always carried with her. It was stuffed full, but she pulled out an old brown photograph stuck to gray cardboard. In it, a little girl with a big hair ribbon on the back of her head sat in a low cart behind a huge, hairy Saint Bernard. It must have been summer, because the dog was panting and the little girl had on a white pinafore with ruffles and pleats. She looked about five years old. Beyond the dog were the feet and legs of a bigger girl, also wearing a white dress. Boots pulled at my sleeve and pointed at the picture. "That's not Aunt Aggie." He looked worried. If this old lady could suddenly be changed into a little girl with a bow, how did he know Bateman Lister III wouldn't find himself an old man with a cane, without ever having gotten to be a cowboy?

"Yes, it is," I said carefully. "It's Aunt Aggie a long, long time ago. Remember when you were a baby and now you're bigger? This is Aunt Aggie before she grew."

"Then whose are that legs?" he asked, pointing again. I turned the picture around so Mrs. Pease could see what he meant.

"Oh, *that.*" And she put a peculiar emphasis on the word *that.* "*That's* my sistuh. She was no good."

Boots nodded his head wisely. "No good," he said. "My daddy's no good. Mama says so."

I caught Mrs. Pease's eye, and we exchanged the look people use when they understand something they aren't going to say out loud. "Well, then, Bobby," said Mrs. Pease, "you and I have somethin' in common. We'll just have to be a little extra to each othuh to make up. Now you come heyuh and see if Aggie can't find you a chocolate."

In all the time I knew her, she never stopped calling Boots "Bobby" or me "Joan," but after that afternoon I didn't mind.

When I had dropped Boots off at his house and gone home, I went out to the garage to help Dad sort books. If you're going to sell used paperbacks, you can't order them from a warehouse, you have to get them from people who've already read them. First we'd gotten everything we could from our friends in Vicinity and all Mom's cousins in Worcester, then Dad had spent a lot of time last summer driving around to yard sales and flea markets while Mother was at work. I hadn't realized until recently just how many books he'd collected. It was when he had gotten discouraged about finding another job, after he was laid off from Data Processing Systems.

I would have enjoyed sorting the books anyway, but it was a special pleasure to do it with Dad now that he was looking forward to the new store.

When we finished up and went outside, the night was breezy and there was a huge moon like a pale tomato. We started up the drive toward our house, which is Victorian, with shingles like snake scales above the first floor and a silly little tower in one corner. In the dark it seemed safe to ask the question that was on my mind. "Dad, how come you went to work for DPS when you liked things with books better?"

We went three steps before he answered. I could hear the difference between the gravel parts and the muddy parts of the driveway under our feet.

Then Dad's big arm came out and wrapped around my head so it was pulled in against his shoulder. Just a few months ago, it seemed, my ear had been at the level of his ribs and I'd been too little to ask questions like that. Or maybe I'd only thought I was.

"Jo, honey, do you know something? People do all sorts of things for the wrong reasons. When I got out of school, everything was computers, computers, computers if you wanted good money and a safe job. For a guy from a not quite poor family who was planning ahead to marrying a cute little accounting major and supporting a daughter and an oversize cat—well, it was just the smart thing to do. I'd always been bright enough. I went to Wang and then to Data Processing, and they wanted me to write software, so I wrote software. It never occurred to me that I just might not be much good at it."

"You were, too, good at it!"

"Jo, that's your mother talking. She's as loyal as Lassie. As far as she's concerned, every sheep in her fold has a golden fleece. But I thought you were the family realist."

We had stopped by the kitchen door. Inside, I could see the back of Mother's blue cable-knit sweater, her neat black curls and the end of Watermelon's tail waving lazily as he lay in her lap. She was "setting up the books" for the store, and Dad and I both knew without looking that she would be smiling slightly as she made columns of headings and figures so tidy, they looked as if they'd been printed.

Dad's voice was louder suddenly, sounded angry. "I hated it, you know, Jo. That's why the layoff hit me so hard. I'd suffered so much in that job, it seemed as if I'd earned the right to keep it."

"Yes," I said. "I know. Until Mother went back to work, I thought all grown-ups hated their jobs."

"And what in the world can I say to that? Jo, you're too young to be so disillusioned. Your mother and I are staking an awful lot on this thing. It's our rebellion against the idea that you can't make a living doing what you like. Don't make up your mind yet about people being happy in their jobs, okay?"

I went to bed and lay awake thinking about our conversation. Probably I should have been resting up for school. On the other hand, there wasn't much in school that I needed to be rested for. I had managed things so well that almost nobody knew I was there.

CHAPTER 4

I think I was in about the third grade when I began to fade into the background in school. I know it was the year we studied protective coloration. I loved the insect that looks like a piece of stick, the nesting bird that pretends to be part of the marsh, and the giraffe whose spots make it look like a sun-dappled tree.

I'd always been tall and not very good at running, but that didn't matter so much because my friend Julie and I were a team. She had a big sister and brother who took karate, and by the time we were in first grade she'd had the most impressive power kick on the playground. Anybody who wanted to push Jo Morse around would have to watch out for

Julie Mantell. We did everything together. We even had the same initials.

Still, I found it useful to practice being like the walkingstick insect. It wasn't that I couldn't defend myself. It was the things I said when I did it. My stuffy uncle Charles told Mother I was a Problem Child, the time when I was five and I said his company's new perfume smelled just like what happens when you put leftover fruit cup down the garbage disposer. And Jimmy Gramling's mother called mine to complain that he was having nightmares the time he wouldn't give back my blue rope belt with the horsehead buckle and I told him it would turn into a big, hairy blue snake with a horse's head and bite off his nose and fingers while he was asleep. It seemed, as I got older, to make much less trouble if I only talked to Julie and her family, younger kids who didn't understand me anyway, and my parents.

Then the Mantells moved to Belmont.

That was the summer after sixth grade. I still wrote to Julie and phoned her and saw her sometimes in the summer, but it wasn't the same. By now, though, I was so used to collecting my good grades in English and social studies, while speaking only when spoken to, that changing would be impossible. It would have been like having one of the desks start chattering away.

Lately, though, things had been happening to make me uncomfortable. Our high school starts in the eighth grade and the teachers up there all seemed to be keen on class participation. In particular, there was a Ms. Melander in social studies. I suspected it was because of her that my mother had given me one of her Serious Talks, in which she said I was too withdrawn and it was time I started "coming out of my shell." When I'd told her turtles only come out of their shells when they're dead and made into soup, she just looked hurt and said she didn't know what to do with me. I felt bad about that, but by now I hoped she and Dad would forget the whole thing in the excitement about the bookstore.

In any case, it made one more reason to spend time with Mrs. Pease: the things she wanted from me were ones I was able to give.

The afternoon after my talk with Dad was the one when Mrs. Pease gave Frosty away. A couple of times since I'd known her, she'd had stray cats for adoption. This one was a silver-point Siamese—a bouncy little guy, but very cuddly and purry too. Mrs. Pease said he liked to suck fingers and "knead bread" with his front claws because he'd been taken away from his mother too soon. Some kids had found him in the woods one cold night and brought him right to Mrs. Pease. For a week or so she'd been trying to find him a home, but she was very particular about the people who answered her ads. Sometimes she turned them down without even meeting them because they didn't "sound nice."

This afternoon, though, Boots and I arrived and found her all excited. A mother and her little girl had driven out from Frontburg to look at Frosty over the weekend, and now they were coming back to take him home. Boots and I helped "Aunt Aggie" get some things together to send with the kitten. She went to the kitchen for a container of turkey and vegetables, and a cellophane package of Tender Vittles. The she pulled open a drawer in her big mahogany sideboard and got out a red leather collar with a bell on it. The drawer seemed to be full of collars, leashes, and harnesses in various sizes and colors. "Now, Joan," she said, "you just run up in my attic and get me some catnip. You'll find a big bunch on a nail by the light pull."

I had never been upstairs in the house before, and as far as I knew, Mrs. Pease never went upstairs herself because of her arthritis. All the rooms had bedroom sets of curly Victorian furniture, with marble-topped washstands and dark old pictures on the walls showing things like the Baby Jesus petting a lamb or a fat little girl hugging a bored-looking collie. All the beds had dust sheets over them, and all the rooms had screen doors on them, as if they had been used for cats, like the kitchen.

I passed a bathroom where a bathtub with claw feet was filled with dusty boxes, and rolls and rolls of what looked like wallpaper nearly hid the toilet. Then I found the way to the attic, where I had just time to glimpse a big dusty space filled with old furniture as I broke off some catnip from a bunch the size of a small bush. Mother has catnip in her herb garden, and I've always loved the smell that's halfway between lemons and marigold leaves. Now I recognized it as one part of the smell that hung around Mrs. Pease's. Camphor was in it, and cats, and stew, as well as catnip and some other things I hadn't identified. It wasn't entirely pleasant, and I was always surprised that Boots, who had a sensitive nose like most little kids, seemed to ignore it.

When I got downstairs, the people from Frontburg were in the parlor patting Frosty and getting ready to put him into the cardboard carrying case Mrs. Pease had ready. The little girl had brought a fuzzy pink doll blanket for him to lie on and was wide-eyed and speechless with excitement over her new pet. I had no idea then how much I was going to hear about that child and her mother and Frosty. At the time, Mrs. Pease just waved them off from the front door with smiles and promises to telephone and "find out how yuh new kitty's gettin' on." Then she seemed suddenly tired and took hold of my arm on the way back to the parlor. She sat down heavily in her big rocker with the spindle back and said to me, "Joan, get me my big book."

"Which one is that?" I asked. I had never known Mrs. Pease to read a book, and the few I had seen in the house sat between marble bookends on top of the china cupboard and had titles like *When Your Pet Dies* and *God Loves All Creatures.*

"Right on the table, with my paypuhs."

Then I saw a big book like a ledger bound in red and green leather, half hidden beneath the stacks of old envelopes, bunches of postcards in rubber bands, paper-napkin boxes stuffed with receipted bills, and back numbers of animal magazines that covered the top of the scallop-edged table. I got it out and brought it over, while Boots began looking at a stack of old-fashioned valentines that had fallen when I moved the book.

"Ain't you nevuh seen this befaw?" Mrs. Pease had to steady the pencil cup beside her with one hand before she could pick a pencil out of it with the other. "These are all my little visituhs. Says who took 'em and wheyuh they went. See heyuh—1956. That's aftuh I was widowed. 'Tootsie, a black and white dog. About 2 yeahs. To Abigail Jenks.' They lived on the old Batchfield place then. Had that little dog fifteen yeahs. And, my land, look at that—'Pearl, white kitten 9 weeks. To Sarah Goodson.' That cat was the grandmothuh of my little Dolly. Young Sally, that's my Billy's sistuh, she come by one day with this bit of a thing in huh pocket. 'Mama wants you to have this one,' she says. 'She thinks it's old Tootsie's last litta.' Pearl was Tootsie's motha. And the old cat died the next spring, sure enough. My, how this does bring it all back." She had tears in her eyes, and I felt the back of my nose getting hot too. Almost thirty years ago. Mrs. Pease's cats really were like family to her. She had known their parents and grandparents, maybe those of their owners too.

"Can I look, Mrs. Pease? How far back does the book go?"

She handed it right over and seemed pleased that I was interested. The first entries in the book weren't dated, but after a few pages she pointed out the heading 1923. "I was just married then, when I stahted my wuhk fuh animals. 'Twas awful then—no sheltuhs and almost no laws to protect 'em, and some people so *cruel,* especially to the hosses. Now you look at this clippin'. Let's see, let's see." She thumbed through the pages. The newspaper clipping she turned to was dated February 4, 1928. "Read it aloud," she commanded.

"Local Woman Reproves Carter," it said. "On Tuesday last, Mrs. Wilson Pease of Vicinity objected strongly to carter William Bowman's beating of his horse when the animal slipped on the ice and fell in front of the First Parish Church. An altercation ensued, in which Mrs. Pease took possession of the whip and threatened to use it on the man if he did not desist from abusing his horse. The event was witnessed by a considerable crowd, which seemed disposed to take sides in the argument. Constable Reeves had to be called to restore order. Mrs. Pease intends to bring the incident to the attention of the Humane Society and urges all horse owners to see that their animals are properly shod and fed if they must work in cold weather. 'It's a crime,' she said, 'the way some people abuse a poor animal that is only doing its best.' "

"My goodness, Mrs. Pease, did you really do that?" I had trouble imagining her young and strong enough to take a whip away from somebody but no trouble at all believing she would do it if she could.

"Did I do it, child? I should say I did. What it don't say theyuh is that I used that whip, too, right where it'd do the most good. 'Twasn't ladylike, so they wouldn't print it in the paypuh, but I allus stood up fuh what I believed in." I looked over and saw that Boots was listening with his eyes the size of silver dollars and patting Thunder's nose as if it were his horse Aunt Aggie had saved right before his eyes.

Mrs. Pease was quiet awhile, looking out her front window and thinking. I turned some more pages in the book. Some of the entries were quite long. People had brought her cats and dogs that were sick or hurt and she had taken care of them. "Sat up all nite with Happy," said one entry, "but the pnumonia was too much for her. She died 6 o'clock." Another one was about a dog named Butch: "Geting around good now. Don't know why that fool doctor said he had to be put down." As the pages went on there were more and more clippings. The City of Lowell gave her an award for raising funds toward a new animal shelter. The president of the Massachusetts Society for the Prevention of Cruelty to Animals named her as an outstanding "citizen volunteer." The Anti-Vivisection League made her its northern Massachusetts representative.

There were dozens of short paragraphs that began something like this: "Blackie, the lovable year-old female cat pictured above, is seeking a good home. Shown here with Mrs. Agnes Cully Pease, who is giving her temporary shelter . . ." and so on. In all, nearly sixty years of taking care of animals other people didn't want.

No, I thought as I helped her write up Frosty's adoption a little later, she's not just a weird old lady. I looked at my own spiky handwriting underneath Mrs. Pease's shaky penciling on the latest page of the book, and I felt I was part of something. Maybe not something terribly big, when you think of people blowing each other up all over the world. Saving a few animals isn't a lot compared to that. But still, it wasn't on the side of the bombs either. In its own way, it was on the right side.

CHAPTER 5

THE next week when we arrived at Mrs. Pease's, she looked awful. Her eyes were red, and at first I thought she had a cold, but then I saw she had been crying. "Don't mind me," she said, "I'm just all upset about my little Frosty. That woman is a *monstuh.*"

"Why, Mrs. Pease, what happened?" I asked, imagining the worst. Boots was looking scared. Not even the friendly monsters on *Sesame Street* have convinced him that dreadful Things with scales and horns aren't hiding just where parents and babysitters can't see them.

We were still standing in the front hall, and Mrs. Pease was leaning against the newel post. She sat down on a stair suddenly and began to rock back and forth as if she hurt inside. "He's bein' *mistreated,* my little kitty. Mistreated bad. Oh, Joanie, what'm I gonna do?" She threw me a sharp look. "Yuh don't drive, do yuh?"

Being tall always makes people think I'm older than I am. "Oh, no. It'll be years and years before I can drive."

"Well, I gotta find someone'll take me to Frontbuhg. I gotta bring him home wheyuh somebody can love him."

"Oh, Mrs. Pease! How do you know they're not being nice to Frosty?"

"*How do I know?* Why, my friend Mrs. Rowe, that's how—lives with huh married daughtuh right downstreet. I sent huh ovuh. Oh! You cahn't trust people, no mattuh how nice they seem. I called that woman right up an' told huh what I thought of huh. But you know? She wouldn't give me my kitty back. That woman hung the phone on me!"

"She hung up on you?"

"Bold as brass. She's a bad one, all right." I was glad to see that Mrs. Pease looked better now that she was fighting mad. The pink was in her cheeks instead of her eyes, and she heaved herself up off the stairway as if she were going for the horsewhip. By the light from the red glass lamp overhead, she looked positively fierce. "You'll see. I'll get my kitty back. If Lily can't take me, I'll *send the Humane after 'em.*"

I said I hoped that would work, and Boots and I left. I was afraid she would start telling us whatever awful things those people were doing to Frosty, and I didn't want Boots to hear. Maybe I didn't want to hear either.

We spent the next afternoon at the store, watching the sign being hung: THE READER'S REBELLION. I had come up with the idea myself, because of what Dad said about rebelling against a job he hated, and Mom and Dad both liked it.

When the sign was up, I had a sort of embarrassed feeling, as if people could tell who had thought it up, just by reading it.

I telephoned Mrs. Pease that night to find out about Frosty and the Humane Society. "They said they'd get right at it," she reported, but a few days later she greeted Boots and me with bad news. "They say they cahn't do a thing! It's all these regulations and such. I think it's wicked, wicked! If only I could go thayuh! I'd give that woman a piece of my mind, all right. But I ain't done yet. I been waitin' fuh you to come so you could dial me that infamation. They talk so's I cahn't unduhstand."

I got the number she wanted and dialed for her. It was the mayor's office in Frontburg. I was amazed when she ended up talking to the mayor himself and called him Johnny. "I want you to send a policeman ovuh and get my kitty back. You know I wuhn't stand fuh cruelty." She gave Frosty's address and the name of the people who had him, but when she hung up she didn't seem too hopeful.

"That Johnny Callan!" she said. "I just don't know. He wouldn't promise a thing—just said he'd 'look into it.' You'd think a big man like that'd have time for a little kitty, even if he was a high muckamuck." She seemed to be getting sad again, so I got her to tell Boots about what it was like to be a little girl in the old days in Vicinity.

By the time we left, I had forgotten all about Frosty, but I was reminded at dinner that night. Dad and Mother were interested in Mrs. Pease and would ask me for the latest, every time I'd been over there. Mother was particularly concerned because she's always had a soft spot for animals. She wouldn't even let me keep caterpillars in a jar when I was little, and now I'm kind of glad.

When I finished my story, Mother surprised me by saying, "I have to drive to the printer's in Frontburg on Saturday, Jo. Would it do any good, do you think, if we took a look at this situation? Maybe, just maybe, we could talk some sense to this woman." I could see Dad making an astonished face at her across the table. It wasn't like her to go getting into other people's problems.

Mother went to get more mashed potatoes from the warm place on the back of the stove. "Hal, I know we probably can't help. But it does sound as if Mrs. Pease has done all she can. Whalen Street is right on my way, anyway."

Dad had picked up Watermelon and was rubbing his big striped belly. "I'm not convinced, but I can see you women are going to have your way. Just remember this: If some unfriendly husband and father greets you at the door with a shotgun, you have absolutely no right to be there or ask anybody anything."

After that, I really hoped the whole affair would be settled by Saturday, but it wasn't. "That Johnny Callan was just stringin' me along." Mrs. Pease sighed. "He ain't gonna do an'thin'. An' to think his fathuh got his fust job from my husband."

I had never heard her mention her husband before. All I knew about him was that he had been called Wilson and died right after the Second World War. There was a framed photograph in the parlor, showing Wilson Pease kneeling by a large collie. She often referred to the dog, whose name had been Toby. Now I asked her what her husband had done. "He wuhked at the wallpaypuh place, ovuh by the ahmy post," she said. And that was all she ever told me on the subject of Wilson Pease.

By the time Saturday came, I was wishing Mother hadn't thought up her plan. No matter what happened, it was bound to be embarrassing. On the other hand, there was Frosty, who was a very dear kitten, with his big ears and his little floppy tail. I couldn't imagine what awful things were being done to him (starved? beaten? locked in a closet?), but each idea that occurred to me was worse than the one before.

My hands were clenched in my lap as we drove up to 64 Whalen Street, and Mother's jaw was set. I knew she wished she hadn't come, but I also knew she wouldn't run away from what she had decided was her duty. In some ways Mother is like Mrs. Pease.

The place was not a house but a rather large three-story apartment building in a dingy section of Frontburg. We got out and went into the tight little hallway where there was a row of metal-fronted mailboxes and buzzers for the tenants.

"There's the name," Mother said to me. "Carmody—three F." I could tell how uneasy she was by the fact that she said something so obvious. I think we had both had the idea we might be able to peek through the windows to see how Frosty was, but now we would have to ring the bell and go in.

"Maybe the Carmodys aren't home," I said.

A door right beside the mailboxes swung suddenly open, and a fat man put his head out. He needed a shave and was wearing a T-shirt that said PLUMBERS DO IT ON THEIR BACKS. "You lookin' fuh Cahmody?" he asked in a loud, hoarse voice. He grinned unpleasantly. "Don't ring. She's just comin' in."

I thought afterward that he must have watched from his window while Mrs. Carmody came down the walk. Certainly he'd timed it so he could see what happened in the hall. The front door was already opening.

Mrs. Carmody had a bag of groceries that seemed too big for her. She was short and thin, with limp, light brown hair spilling out from under a fuzzy knitted hat. She hadn't seen us because the bag was blocking her view, and when Mother said uncertainly, "Mrs. Carmody?" she jumped and put her back against the closed door.

"Oh, no. You're not from Mrs. Pease again?"

She looked terrified, and the super (if that's what the fat man was) seemed to be enjoying the scene as much as a ball game. Mother said, "Well, we did think—" but Mrs. Carmody interrupted her.

"Now you just wait a minute!" she said, pushing herself forward and holding on to the groceries as if they were a shield. "This time you're going to come up and see. I can't stand any more of this, I really can't. You come up, right now. Yes, come up!" She was pushing us in front of her and there was nowhere to go but up the stairs. Behind us, the super kept his door open until it was obvious he wasn't going to overhear anything else.

"Don't you go anywhere," warned Mrs. Carmody as she groped for her keys. "Don't you go a single foot." Her hand shook, and I began to be afraid she was crazy instead of angry. She pushed open the door of an apartment that seemed to be nothing but a tiny kitchen and one room. There wasn't much furniture, but it was tidy except for a few toys on the floor. Mrs. Carmody dumped the groceries on the table and clenched her hands to stop them from shaking.

"First it was that awful old woman with the purple hair. Then that man from the Humane Society, and Suzie cried all night. Thank God she's at her friend's house now. And then a policeman from the *mayor*!" We were just standing there while she paced up and down.

"Let me tell you about my Suzie and that kitten. It's the only thing she's got, since the divorce. My husband quit on me, left us nothing. We lost the house and most of the furniture, had to give our dog away. He was too big for an apartment like this. Suzie loved that dog—she's just in kindergarten. She didn't understand. So I thought a kitten, an extra-special kitten, you know, Siamese. I couldn't believe it when I saw the ad. And Mrs. Pease seemed so nice at first . . ."

I heard noises from the kitchen and slipped out to see what they were. Mrs. Carmody didn't notice. She was appealing to Mother. "You can understand, can't you?" she said more quietly. "We do the best we can for him. I know this isn't the Ritz. But sometimes I worry that I can't even get milk for Suzie . . ."

I had found out who was playing with a spoon in the kitchen sink, and came back with Frosty in my arms. He was a little fatter than he had been two weeks ago, and he was managing his feet better. I put my face down in his soft, vanilla-colored fur because I didn't want to look at Mrs. Carmody. She seemed to notice me for the first time. "Why, you're the girl that was at Mrs. Pease's that day! Ohhh. You're friends of hers, and you won't believe me either." Tears started to run down her face, and I saw she was really young, not much older than somebody in high school.

Then Mother had her arm around Mrs. Carmody and was sitting her down in a chair. "There's been a misunderstanding," she said. "Just a misunderstanding. Jo, honey, go in the kitchen and make some tea." I went, but couldn't find anything except instant coffee, so I made two cups of that, one for Mrs. Carmody and one for me. I thought I needed it, and Mother hates instant.

By the time I got back, Mrs. Carmody and Mother were calling each other Mary and Louisa, and Mrs. Carmody had dried her face and even put on some lipstick. "I'm sorry," she was saying, "I sort of went to pieces. Suzie just *can't* lose Frosty now. I told Mrs. Pease. He sleeps in her arms, and she hasn't had the nightmares since we got him. But all Mrs. Pease talks about is getting him back. She—she *threatened to sue me.*" She looked as if she might cry again.

Mother turned around and gave Frosty a long, measuring look, as if he were a column of figures that needed adding up. He was lying on his back in my lap now, playing with a button on my jacket, and he looked just as happy and healthy as any kitten ought to look.

"Mary," said Mother, "just what was it Mrs. Pease—and her friend with the purple hair—thought was wrong with Frosty?"

"Why, didn't you know? It was the food, mostly. She didn't want me to feed him canned food, and I told her I wouldn't. I mean, I thought I'd keep her happy. I didn't know she had, like, spies. And then there was the view."

"The *view*?"

"Yes, that woman who came said he had to have something to look out at—birds or something, and of course—" I followed her gesture toward the window and saw that it faced a wall about twenty feet away, across a dim courtyard. I doubted Frosty would care. I had already seen what was *inside* the apartment—the crumpled paper toy on a string tied to the back of a chair, the empty box of Pampers made into a bed with a soft pink doll's blanket inside, the red jacks ball in the middle of the floor. And of course the food and water dishes in the kitchen.

"Can you tell her?" asked Mrs. Carmody. "Can you explain?"

Mother was looking at me. "I don't know," I said. "I don't think—I mean, she may not listen."

"But you'll try?" pleaded Mrs. Carmody. "Please try. She likes you. She'll pay attention to you."

For the millionth time, I wished I were small and useless-looking. "I'll tell her Frosty seems fine," I promised, "but I doubt if she'll change her mind."

We said good-bye then and went back to the car in silence. It took me by surprise when Mother began to laugh as she drove off down Whalen Street. "What a pair of fools we looked! Going to save the poor, abused kitten! Oh, my goodness!"

Then I started to laugh too.

CHAPTER 6

For the next several days Boots and I stayed away from Mrs. Pease's. I felt very glad she didn't know about our afternoon in Frontburg. That meant I had to find extra-interesting things for Boots to do so he wouldn't ask for Aunt Aggie. I even spent quite a few of my own quarters on the plastic "gallopy horse" in front of the supermarket, but we both knew it was not the same as Thunder.

I told myself I was hoping Mrs. Pease would forget all about Frosty and things would go back to the way they were, but actually I was the one who couldn't forget. I had felt foolish, and so had Mother, although we laughed about it, and we had both seen the little twinkle in Dad's eye that meant "I thought so," but that he was much too nice to put into words. What kind of a person, I asked myself, could really be saving animals that needed help and at the same time get all upset over one that didn't need saving?

I wasn't too pleased, therefore, when Mrs. Pease telephoned me a few evenings later. I'm not good at telephones anyway. Talking to people I can't see makes me nervous, and one thing I can never do on the telephone is say no—to invitations or people selling magazines, or whatever. Mrs. Pease told me, not asked me, to come over after school the next day. "Thayuh's a stray cat around," she said. "I seen him two–three times, ovuh to Bensons'. I want yuh to catch him fuh me."

"But, Mrs. Pease, I—I don't know how to catch a cat. A strange one, I mean."

"Don't worry." She sounded quite cheerful. "A smaht gel like you, Joan—you'll catch on." She hung up before I could think of any excuses.

I still hadn't thought of any when Boots and I knocked at her door the next afternoon.

Mrs. Pease was a good general. She had her weapons all lined up in the front hall, ready for me. "Now, yuh not gonna get him the fust day. He's a big old tommy and he's smaht. I been watchin' him. He's livin' unduh the back o' that shed, downstreet." She pointed toward the corner, where you could just see one end of the Benson House's toolshed through the bare branches of some shrubs.

The Benson House is one of the biggest and nicest

in Vicinity, built right on the corner of Main and Oak streets by a former governor of Massachusetts. It's owned now by the Society for the Preservation of Something-or-other, but they only keep it open in the summer. Not even the caretaker would be going around the toolshed at this time of year. No paths were shoveled through the two-week-old snow.

"What you want to do," Mrs. Pease instructed, "is give him some food and let him get to know yuh. Every time yuh go, take this carry-case and this blanket, so he'll get used to 'em. Then one day, he'll come up to get his food and *pff*—you got him." She made a rolling motion with the hand that wasn't holding on to the doorjamb, and I realized she meant me to wrap the cat in a blanket, the way we have to with Watermelon before we give him a pill.

It was a horrid day with a damp, mean wind blowing over soggy snow. Boots and I went off down the street, he in his little red snowsuit that makes him look like a Christmas elf, and I in my jeans and parka, wishing I were half as warm as he was.

The snow between the sidewalk and the toolshed was deep enough so that I had to carry Boots, which was awkward, considering the plastic dish of cat stew, blanket, and carrying case. I was looking around for cat tracks, not finding any, and thinking I would give the whole thing up except that I knew Mrs. Pease was watching from her front window.

At the far corner of the shed was a hole between two foundation stones, and cat tracks leading toward the trees at the edge of the lawn. At least Mrs. Pease hadn't imagined the cat. I was down on my heels setting out the food dish, when Boots announced, "Kitty's in there, an' he's mad." He had his face down by the dark hole, and now even I could hear the *rrRRow, rrRRow* noise that a cat makes when it's warning anything and anybody to keep away. I squatted down beside Boots and saw a pair of furious yellow eyes and two torn ears pressed nearly flat against a big square yellow head. I decided it would be a long time before I picked *that* poor stray cat up in a blanket, but I left the food, returned the other things to Mrs. Pease, and took Boots away to the library for the afternoon story hour and cookies.

By the time it was dark, the damp, mean wind had gotten stronger and colder, and by bedtime we were having the winter's first real blizzard. It seemed as if the whole sky had simply turned to snow and was falling on Vicinity so fast that in the morning there would be nothing left but a smooth white plain where the town had been and a great black hole where the sky had been.

I've always liked the big storms that stop traffic and seem to take you back a couple of hundred years to the time when people did things with their own feet and hands. We had lots of firewood in the cellar, lots of flour and cornmeal and beans in the pantry, lots of birdseed in a sack on the porch, and plenty of hamburger in the freezer. We had snow shovels and warm boots for going out with, and we had books and jigsaw puzzles for staying in with. We also had candles and kerosene lamps, and I half hoped the electricity would go off so we could all read and tell stories by firelight like Abraham Lincoln. Even with the lights on, the storm was fun at our house. It was obvious there wouldn't be any school the next day, so instead of facing up to the English paper that was due Friday, I went into the living room, where we had a fire in the Franklin stove, and listened to Dad reading aloud the part about the blizzard in *The Long Winter.* I even managed to feel a little glad that we didn't live miles from anywhere in a house made of sod and logs, lost on a prairie as wide as the sea, the way Laura and Mary do in the book.

Knowing I didn't have to get up in the morning made it hard for me to fall asleep. My bedroom is really the best room in the house, everybody says so, because of the funny little round tower built onto one corner of it, with a big, thick cushion on the circular window seat that runs around underneath its windows. It's a cold place because no storm windows will fit there, but I put on my long quilted bathrobe and sat looking out at the snow. Watermelon, of course, had made himself into a lap robe and that helped a lot. It's amazing how warm a twenty-four-pound cat can be.

That made me think of the other cat, the one under the Benson House toolshed. No matter how unfriendly he acted, he didn't deserve to be snowed in and starve to death. I decided to go and see him again tomorrow, even if I had to bring him *canned* cat food like Watermelon's.

It would make a good horror story, I thought, told from the cat's point of view. There he is, starving and freezing in the dark, while all around him he can hear signs of life—children laughing, big, well-fed dogs trotting by, even the birds fighting over sunflower seeds in people's backyards. You could write it like Edgar Allan Poe and have him die slowly in the end. Or you could tell it in short sentences without any adjectives, like a TV reporter, and it would turn out to be society's fault that the cat died, because nobody cared.

I hadn't intended to think about anything like school at all, but imagining the cat story made me worry about Mr. Stropner.

Mr. Stropner is one of the best and most popular teachers in the Vicinity school system. Everybody in school knows that, and most of the kids even agree with it, just the way everybody knows to stay out of Mrs. Amory's class because she did her teacher training during the War of 1812 and the only thing she hates more than sixth-grade boys is sixth-grade girls. Fortunately, I never had Mrs. Amory, but Mr.

Stropner was lying in wait for me, and until I was actually in his class, I didn't even know he was a trap.

Parents love Mr. Stropner because he won an award for teaching kids who can't write how to get good scores on their English competency tests. He's keen on what he calls "workable prose," and he has all kinds of cute little tricks for helping people remember not to split infinitives and when *i* comes before *e*. He's a tall, thick man with black hair that makes an *M* at the top of his forehead, and he talks in a loud voice and smiles all the time, even when he's handing back papers with bad grades. He coaches hockey, and treats English class a little as if it were the regional playoffs. Every time somebody writes a sentence that begins with a capital and ends with a period, it's as if the team had made a goal on the play. Maybe I would like him, too, if I didn't know the difference between a noun and a verb.

My problem with Mr. Stropner is not "workable prose," however. My problem is that Mr. Stropner doesn't like my attitude—although about what, I'm not sure. It certainly isn't my attitude in class, because I've been careful not to have one. However, Mr. Stropner never leaves anybody alone. He likes to say he plans to know every one of us "inside and out" before the year is over, but when I write what's inside me, he doesn't like it. For one thing, Mr. Stropner doesn't want you to write anything that might not be true. I don't mean lies, I mean descriptions. He wants everybody to write the kind of "workable prose" you need to get a job or go through college.

I think Mr. Stropner would rather no one was allowed to write poetry or stories, and he certainly never assigns them, but there's a school rule that you can do "creative writing" instead of the standard homework a couple of times a year. That's where I made my first mistake. Instead of an essay on "If I Ran the School," I handed in a poem about the Vicinity town dump. The dump is a huge, creepy area dotted with piles of sand, gravel, and junk in different categories like metal, appliances, tires, brush, and trash. I wrote a poem in which the old, abandoned furniture is telling stories about houses and families to the rats in the moonlight and the old tires are singing about the roads they've been on, and Mr. Stropner gave me a D on it.

I never talk to teachers, but I went up and asked him if he'd like me to rewrite the poem so it rhymed, and he said no and gave me a list of what was wrong with the poem. Mr. Stropner thinks lists are clear and concise, which means they are workable prose. This was his list: 1. Poor choice of subject. 2. Vague, metaphorical language. 3. Unclear transitions. 4. Anthropomorphism. I had to look that last one up, and I discovered it means Mr. Stropner thinks I don't know that chairs and tires can't really speak. I was so upset that I let Jenny Carson catch me trying not to cry in the girls' room, and for some reason she knew it was about Mr. Stropner. She acts all right to me, or maybe she's only the kind of person who's nice to everybody. "Listen, Jo," she said in her soft voice, not as if she wanted to be superior, "next time, if you *have* to write a poem, just write about spring."

"Spring?" I was too amazed to pretend not to care.

"Sure. Or the birds at the bird feeder, or the sunset over Boston. Something pretty."

"But the sun doesn't set over Boston. We're west of it."

"I know. But old Jock Strap won't. My sister had him two years ago."

No matter how much I thought about it now, though, I couldn't see any way to get out of writing goody-goody English papers for the rest of the year. I can stand a C or two, but D's make parents nervous.

By now I had completely lost my cozy, snowed-in mood. I told myself firmly I would be like Scarlett O'Hara in *Gone with the Wind* and think about that tomorrow. I got into bed and remembered to lie on my side so I didn't have to notice the way my toes were threatening to bump the footboard if I lay straight.

CHAPTER 7

THE next morning, we found out the storm had been just as big as it seemed. The plows had not gotten to Deming Street at all. Snow lay level from sidewalk to sidewalk, except for two deep tracks that had been made by some big, heavy truck with chains. We couldn't go out at first because drifts blocked both doors when we tried to open them. I had to climb out one of the kitchen windows and scrape the door clear before Dad and I could shovel the walk. Then a friend of Mother's called and told us not even to try to go to the store—the electricity was out on that whole side of town. "Everything east of the fire station" was what people were saying. Only Main Street was plowed, and both the supermarket and the post office were closed.

It was like a holiday, so Dad made waffles in the big, old-fashioned waffle iron that had belonged to Grandpa Morse. I was watching the way the batter creeps and oozes out between the two halves, like something in a science fiction movie, when Mom asked, "Jo, how does Mrs. Pease heat her house?"

"Heat it? I don't know."

"Well, think, hon. What kind of radiators does she have?"

Around here, everybody talks a lot about winter heat. People go on about forced hot water, hot air, natural gas, fuel oil, pea coal, radiant electric, spot heating, and wood furnaces until you can't help remembering some of it. "Well," I said, "there's a thermostat. She asks me to turn it up sometimes. And there are those big silver radiators, the kind that look like accordions. I guess that means hot water."

"Probably," agreed Dad. "It also means she has a furnace that won't work without electricity. Most of them have electric starters. Do you think there's anybody watching out for her? She can't stay in a house with no heat, however many warm, furry bodies there are."

"She doesn't get along with her neighbors, if that's what you mean. Mrs. Robb is almost as old as she is, I think, and Mrs. Pease says she throws trash in her yard—Mrs. Robb does, I mean. The other side is the Walterses. I never see them, but Mrs. Pease says they drink."

"Well, if that's the case, I think you and I had better find out if she's all right. Cold can be dangerous for old people."

As soon as the waffles were eaten, Dad and I started over to Mrs. Pease's with our snow shovels. We were a little worried by then, because Dad had made me telephone and I got a recording saying the phone had been disconnected. We walked down the truck tracks in the center of Deming Street, but had to churn through new snow after we turned onto Fair Street. Oak Street was plowed by now, however, and people were out shoveling, playing, or digging out their cars.

When we got to Mrs. Pease's, we had to shovel before we could even knock. We were nearly up to the little front porch, with its big bird feeder, spooled wooden railings, and sagging floorboards, when we heard a tapping, and there was Mrs. Pease at the parlor window. I could see she had on a thin nylon nightgown trimmed with droopy lace and a fuzzy blue bathrobe with a satin flower sewed on the collar. "Joan!" she shrilled. "What you doin' heyuh?"

Dad stepped up behind me and said in his most polite voice, "How do you do, Mrs. Pease? I'm Johanna's father, Hal Morse. We knew your electricity was out, and we wondered if there was anything we could do. Do you have heat?"

"Electricity? Why, I didn't notice. I've got my

stove, you know; that buhns coal. I don't tuhn the fuhnace on except fuh comp'ny. No, my little family and I are all well and happy." Her faded eyes twinkled in a way I'd never seen before. "Now don't you go worryin' about *me.* A fine, big man like you got othuh things to do than fret ovuh old Aggie." She put her head on one side and smiled at Dad again, and I almost thought she was flirting with him. "My boy Billy'll be ovuh this forenoon to do the walk and get me some coal," she added.

"Well, I'm glad to hear you're all right, Mrs. Pease," Dad said. "Jo telephoned you earlier and got some sort of recording."

"Oh, that! I'll get that straightened 'round once my check comes in. They nevuh leave it off but a few days. Now, Joan"—suddenly she was all businesslike. "How you comin' with that kitty?"

"I'm taking care of him," I said uneasily.

"That's good. Theyuh's not many of us will stand up fuh animals. Well," she said with a little wave of her hand, "I wuhn't keep you." She put her head in and shut the window with a thump.

As we went back down Oak Street, I saw Dad was grinning. "I thought you didn't like Mrs. Pease much," I said.

"You mean because she got you to do her dirty work for her? Well, no. But now that I've met her, I'm glad. You don't find them like that anymore."

"You mean I should go on seeing her?"

"I never said you shouldn't. You might learn a lot

from her. On the other hand, she'll try to tie you up tighter and tighter, the old spider, until you can't get out of her web at all."

After that conversation, I wasn't sure just *how* Dad felt about Mrs. Pease.

I went to check on the cat around noontime, and was glad to find he wasn't really snowed in. Even though the drifts were right up over the foundations of the toolshed, I could see a place where he had just burrowed and bucked his way out until he was under the bushes where the snow was shallower. I assumed he was gone, but when I put down the cat food, I saw a battered yellow head inside the entrance hole. The cat crouched, watching me. He was a long-haired cat, and his yellow fur was matted with cockleburs and tickseed. He had a cut over one eye that made his eyelid droop, and the edges of his ears were as ragged as if someone had snipped at them with pinking shears. He looked tough and mean, but also very hungry. He never took his eyes off the food, and when I stepped back away from it, I almost thought he would come out and start eating. He didn't, though, and it occurred to me that he'd rather not have to eat in the open, where another cat or a dog might try to steal his food. I went back, picked up the dish, and shoved it inside his front door. He bounced back the minute I came near, but he was at the food before I had gotten halfway to the sidewalk. He acted as if he could have eaten twice as much.

I spent the afternoon building a big snow fort with some of the neighborhood kids. They were all younger than I was, and pretty soon I'd be too old for them. I knew I'd have to do something before then—about my life and my attitude and Mr. Stropner and so on. It seemed I was growing *out of* being a kid without knowing what I was growing *into.*

As I headed home my ankles were wet from the snow in the tops of my boots, my ribs were sore where nine-year-old Dewey Zelinger had jumped on me by mistake, and though I'd really had a great time with that fort, working and laughing and rolling little kids over to tickle them, I began to feel cold and discouraged. That's probably why, after I'd had some hot cocoa, I got out some cat food and headed for the Benson House again. That old cat wasn't a cute little thing, either. He must have mewed on dozens of doorsteps hoping for a handout, and gotten yelled or barked at. No wonder he snarled at the world.

It was that quick-falling December dark time, when the shine of the streetlights looks pale and useless and the snow that was so bright goes flat and gray. I squatted down by the hole to look for the cat, but nothing stared at me from the dark. Disappointed, I picked up the empty dish and put down the can.

Then something bumped me from behind and I almost tipped forward onto my knees as the cat dashed around my left side and buried his nose in the can. His haunches were pressed right against me as he ate, and I could feel his body jerk with each gulp. Then I heard a hoarse sound like a rusty motor. No doubt about it—the cat was purring. I sat there, not daring to move, until he was almost done. then I remembered why I was doing all this and began, very quietly, to unzip my parka. I wiggled out of one sleeve, then the other, and dropped it over him just as he was giving the can a last, loving lick. I wasn't quick about it, and he could certainly have run away if he'd tried. Instead, all he did was poke his head out of the fabric and rub hard against me as I held him close to my shoulder.

He didn't weigh as much as I'd expected. I put my gloved hand down and grabbed his back feet so he couldn't gouge my stomach if he changed his mind, but he only dug his front claws hard into my shoulder to hang on. I was sorry then that I hadn't brought Mrs. Pease's blanket; I was wearing just one sweater and a T-shirt and his claws went right through them.

I wrapped my other arm over his shoulders, and began to carry the cat toward the sidewalk, half expecting him to struggle and me to lose some skin. Instead, I felt his big old head pushing and pushing against my neck under my jaw and heard the rusty purr again. This cat certainly wasn't sorry to be "caught."

As I went, stepping carefully in my own boot tracks, I thought maybe I would take the cat to my house instead of Mrs. Pease's. This guy really liked me and I was getting to like him too. Then I remembered what Watermelon would probably think about a big yellow tomcat's invading his territory, and that tomcats, even house-trained ones, spray urine indoors. I didn't think my mother would be very pleased at that prospect. Besides, I was freezing without my parka, and Mrs. Pease's house was a lot closer than my own.

As we went past the corner of Main and Oak, a black Labrador came bounding out of a garage to bark at us. The cat gave a lunge, and I would have lost him if I hadn't had his back feet in my hand. As it was, I was pretty sure my shoulder and neck were shredded. I yelled at the dog, and a man in a sheepskin coat came out of the garage, scolded the dog, and called to me, "It's okay, he won't hurt you."

"I know," I said, "but I've got a stray cat here." The dog had retreated a little, but the cat was vibrating in my arms as if he were going to blast off any minute.

The man came up and grabbed the dog's collar. "Oh," he said, "you going up to Aggie Pease's?"

"Uh-huh."

"Well, I guess it's good to get them off the street.

All the same, it's a shame about that place, you know?"

"Yeah," I muttered, "I know." He hauled the dog back, I tightened my grip on the cat, and we went on up the block.

When I got there, I could see that someone, maybe her "boy" Billy, had finished the shoveling and filled the bird feeder. The porch light was on, but by the time she answered my knock the cat was getting restless and I was starting to shiver.

Mrs. Pease was delighted to see the cat. She fussed over him and insisted on my coming in. Then she began trying to give me something again. She had done it once or twice before, offering me a little china vase or a carved wooden napkin ring, but I had always said no. The idea embarrassed me and I had no use for the things anyway. This time, it was a "whatnot"—a little wooden corner shelf with curly edges that hung by the door to the parlor. It was a nice shelf, but that was all the more reason for me not to let her give it to me. I said I really couldn't and at last she gave up. "You'll get it in the end, you'll see. I'll put you down for it in my will."

"Your *will*?" I think I squawked it.

"Of cawse, child, my will." She gave me a sideways glance. "You don't think Aggie's goin' to live forevuh, do you? I'm seventy-three, you know. I could go any time. A lotta nice things I got in this house, too, an' there's plenty that want 'em an' some that ain't gonna get 'em. Why shouldn't I see they'll go whayuh I want 'em to?"

At that moment she looked exactly like the old spider Dad had called her, and I said, "Mrs. Pease, I think you're very nice to think of it, but I really don't want your things. I caught that cat for you because he was cold and hungry.

"I have to go now, I have school tomorrow," I added. I ducked out the door, but a backward glance showed me the expression on her face. It was not a disappointed frown, but a small, satisfied smile.

CHAPTER 8

ABOUT two evenings later I came home and found a note stuck in the kitchen door. My parents were down at the store, getting ready for the Grand Opening, which was only a week or so away, but the note was not in Mom's or Dad's writing. Shaky black pencil letters said *Come and see me right away.* The last two words were underlined twice. Since Mrs. Pease's phone still wasn't working, I supposed I'd have to go. She must have been watching for me, because she threw open the door almost as soon as I'd knocked. "You saved that kitty's life!" she burst out.

"What?"

"You saved his life! Lily took him to the vet this

aftuhnoon—fuh his shots, and a shampoo, and to have his operation, you know—and he was *blocked*!"

"He was what?"

"He was blocked. His urine was blocked. They get that, the tommies. Doctuh said he'd of been dead by tomorruh!"

"You mean the big yellow cat? My cat? He was sick? He looked okay when I found him."

"Yes, they caught it in time, doctuh said, 'Cystitis,' that's the name fuh it. *Oh,*" she went on, "it just makes me cry to think of him out thayuh sick, with no one to watch out fuh him."

It seemed the cat had been in even worse danger than I'd imagined in my unwritten story. "Well," I said, trying to reassure her, "he's all better now." Without thinking about it, I put my arm around her shoulders. Her bones felt as thin as a kitten's. I didn't know what I'd do if she really started crying, so I said as cheerfully as I could, "I know Dr. Kantor will take good care of him. Maybe I'll go over there tomorrow. The animal hospital is right near school."

Mrs. Pease gave a twitch, almost as if I had pinched her. "Dr. Kantuh?" she said. "Oh, I'd nevuh take one of my babies to him. You don't let him at youh kitty, do you?"

I could see trouble coming, so I said half truthfully, "Oh, Watermelon's very healthy, he hardly ever has to go to the vet."

"Well don't you evuh go to that man," said Mrs. Pease severely. "Do you know what he *does*?"

"Does? No."

Mrs. Pease lowered her voice to a hoarse whisper. "He's a *vivisectuh.* He cuts up paw helpless animals in his basement!"

"What for?" I asked, startled.

"Why, fuh *research*!" she said, making it sound like a dirty word. "Them doctuhs does experiments on paw, helpless little animals. Why don't they do 'em on themselves, that's what I'd like to know?"

A couple of months ago I might have listened more closely. Now I thought of fat, kind Dr. Kantor and his blind Samoyed, Sheila, whom Dr. Kantor has refused to "put away" after she got hurt and her owners didn't want a disabled dog. I guessed that Dr. Kantor was just another bee in Mrs. Pease's bonnet, to use one of her own expressions. All I said was "That sounds awful. What doctor *do* you send your animals to?"

Fortunately, she seemed willing to take up the conversation where it had been before vivisection got mentioned. "My animals all go to Dr. Finnegan, in Frontbuhg. That man is a saint, I tell *you.* He saved my old Tip's life when he was at *death's daw.* I had him in to the Angell Memorial in Boston, and they give up on 'em. But Dr. Finnegan, he knew just what 'twas and he fixed that doggie up fine. He lived to eighteen, Tip did, and nevuh had a bit of trouble aftuh." She gave me a triumphant look, as if Tip's good health was proof that all other vets were fiends. I still wanted to know about the yellow cat, however. I was beginning to feel that he was mine in a way. After all, I'd saved his life. She had gone off into her dining room, saying there was something she wanted to get. I began thinking about a name for a tough old yellow cat who had really been around—Hobo, maybe, or Vagabond.

Mrs. Pease came thumping back. She had a dark rectangle in her hand, about the size of a piece of notebook paper. She came close to me and held it out. "I want yuh to have this, Joan," she said, "and I wuhn't take no for an ansuh."

I turned the thing right side up and saw it was a framed picture. Two pink-cheeked little children in dress-up Red Cross caps were solemnly bandaging the paw of a cocker spaniel puppy. Beside them was a battered doll with her plaster arm in a sling. The frame was carved wood with oak leaves and acorns on it. I thought the picture was pretty icky, really, and I wondered how the children's mother was going to get all that adhesive off the puppy's paw, but I knew that this time I couldn't refuse Mrs. Pease's present. It was her way of thanking me for saving the cat, and she wouldn't understand if I told her it had been private between me and him. I said what a cute picture it was and that I had homework.

The temperature was in the twenties outside and there was a wind like a carving knife. I was warm all the way home, though, thinking about a beat-up old cat who would have died except for me, remembering his rusty purr and his claws kneading my shoulder. He'd be back from the vet on Monday, Mrs. Pease had said. I thought I'd bring him a big piece of haddock.

I didn't see Dad and Mother until the next morning at breakfast, they'd stayed so late at the store. I was feeling grumpy, thinking about the "workable prose" on worm farming I had written for Mr. Stropner the night before. I had actually found a book on the subject filed under General Nonfiction in the store and decided the topic was so dull, it would have to be a success with Stropner. "Protein from earthworms," I had written, "was considered tasty eating, when properly prepared, by 55.7% of those tested. What the others said can only be guessed at." I was wondering whether Mr. S. had ever heard the rhyme, "Nobody loves me, everybody hates me,/Goin' out in the garden an' eat worms, worms, worms," when Mom looked up over *The Boston Globe.* "By the way," she said, "I've got some information for Mrs. Pease. I called Loraine Cormier's office—she's our state representative. All Mrs. Pease has to do is send in a form saying she's over sixty-five and lives alone, and they can't turn her phone off because of a couple of late payments. You and Boots can go by the phone office this afternoon and pick up the form for her."

I wasn't eager to go to the phone office, but I went, partly because Mrs. Pease thought I was a cat savior and partly because it made up a little for what happened with my worm paper. Mr. Stropner didn't even wait a day to give it back. Right after lunch it was on my desk with a C minus on it and the comment *Too flippant. This was a research paper, not a humorous essay.*

Nobody loves me . . .

CHAPTER 9

ALMOST as soon as it opened, the bookstore became one of my favorite places for reading and people-watching. There was a corner beside Science Fiction that was just right. ("For every five math problems, I get a chapter of Arthur C. Clarke.") I even brought in a cushion from my room at home, and Mother thought it was such a good idea, she got some more at a church fair and left them around for people to sit on.

One Saturday in early January, I was vaguely aware that an older woman had come in and was asking about gothic novels, when I heard Dad introducing her to another customer as Lily Lisle. I peeked around the corner at her. Mrs. Lisle had carefully curled gray hair, pink cheeks, and china earrings in the shape of forget-me-nots. Her eyes were sparkling brown and she had a charming way of putting her head on one side when she talked to you, as if she expected you to say something clever and didn't want to miss it. Dad called back to me to ask what had happened to a stack of Mary Stewart novels that had just come in. When she heard my name, Mrs. Lisle turned and chirped, "Morse! Jo Morse! Why, *you* must be Joan."

"Joan? Yes, I guess I am, and you—you must be Mrs. Pease's friend Lily, the one who drives."

"Indeed I am. So you're Aggie's Joan. I've been hearing about you for months, but I was never sure whether your last name was Morse or Moss. And then, she hardly calls anyone by the right name. She gave me the idea you were much older. Well! Isn't it nice that we've met? You know, Aggie doesn't like her friends to be too well acquainted."

She smiled at me as if we were *very* well acquainted, and the way she did it made me feel as if we were. "Hal," she went on, "I hope you know what a lot Jo has done for Aggie Pease. There are so many things I can't help with since I had my little attack, and of course she's quarreled with Beatrice Langley and Ida Frame and those people. I think Agnes is very lucky to have somebody useful and sensible like Johanna. A good student, too, though much too quiet in class, I hear."

I must have gaped at her, because she gave a little chuckle and her eyes sparkled just like Boots's when he has a secret. "Oh, my dear, I'm sorry, I should have explained. Rhonda Melander is my daughter. We chat sometimes about her students since I used to be in the same line of work. I told her to watch out for you because the Morses are all alike—more to them than meets the eye."

I was too astonished to speak, but Mrs. Lisle, the mother of my social studies teacher, wasn't through with me. As she was leaving with her stack of books, she remarked, "You know, dear, I don't know whether you've thought of this, but Aggie Pease would be a wonderful subject for the special oral history project Rhonda is doing next term. You'd make quite a contribution if you interviewed her, and I believe she'd be delighted to cooperate. All those animals, and she does love to talk about them . . ."

That is why I found myself, on the first day of the next term, signing up for Ms. Melander's special local-history project. It was against my policy of never doing anything to get myself noticed, but I knew when I was beaten. And it was a research project, not a discussion group. Besides, Melander was the most interesting teacher I had that term. She might have gotten me in the end without Mrs. Lisle's help, or my mother's. The truth was, ever since I found out about the scrapbook, I had been wanting to see more of it. Mrs. Pease could be kind and selfish, bossy and generous, scheming and forthright, sentimental and hard as nails. Which was the real Aggie Pease: the one that publicly stood up to a man who was beating his horse, the dotty old lady who thought it was cruel that a kitten didn't have a nice view out the window, or even the intolerant old person who still talked about getting a "Jew lawyuh" to sue poor Mrs. Carmody and would name a black cat Niggy? Maybe that scrapbook would tell me.

But though one part of me wanted to show what I could do, another was planning how I could bury myself in Mrs. Pease's records and avoid the rest of the kids in the group.

The next afternoon, Boots and I went over to Mrs. Pease's to see what she thought of my project and ask whether she would cooperate. I was surprised to discover how disappointed I would feel if she said no.

We had not quarreled over Frosty because she was so pleased about my "rescuing" the yellow cat and because she simply dismissed my remark that he seemed fine. "Oh, you don't know an'thin' about it" was all she said.

The first thing we saw when we came in the door that day was the tomcat. I had been so involved with Ms. Melander and the project that I'd almost forgotten him. His coat was clean and fluffy, free of burrs and mats, his claws had been clipped (as I discovered when he biscuited on my hand), and the cut over his eye was just a shiny pink line in the fur. His ears were still ragged, the skin on his nose and lips was still freckled with dark spots, and his muzzle was still pushed in like an old prize fighter's, but he looked healthy and very pleased with himself. "That's my Goldie," said Mrs. Pease. "Ain't he a booful big boy, now?"

Goldie!

I swallowed hard and went on scratching him under the chin. After all, he was her cat really. I would just have to look at him and know that his true name was Hobo. I was about to bring up the history project, but Mrs. Pease had something else on her mind.

By now, we were sitting in the parlor in our usual chairs—she in the spindle-back rocker padded with assorted cushions, shawls, and towels, I on the little settee opposite. Boots was petting Thunder and giving him a fuzzy Life Saver he had unstuck from his pocket.

"My phone is back," said Mrs. Pease, "and oh, Joan, I'm so glad to have it." There were tears in her eyes. "The man rung up to say they'd put it back, and he was so *polite.* You must've given him a real piece of youa mind. You're a good, kind gel, Joan, to take trouble fuh an old woman."

I told her it was really Mom who found out about the form, but she'd made up her mind that I had defeated the phone company single-handed. It made it harder for me to talk about the project. What if she only said yes because she was grateful? When I finally brought it up, I got all twisted in my words, trying to explain that it would be okay if she didn't want to, but of course maybe she'd enjoy it, but on the other hand, it was a lot of time, and not even telling her what the project was. I should have known Mrs. Pease better.

All she said was "Well, I swan. You sayin' you want to write a piece about me? Go ahead and do yuh wuhst." She shook her white curls and gave me a teasing glance. "You wun't tell all Aggie's secrets, now, will you?"

"Oh, no," I promised, "that's part of the project. We have to protect the privacy of our sources." *Besides,* I thought, *I don't suppose she has any secrets.*

By the end of the next week I was beginning to wish that Mrs. Pease had said no to the project. I had forty-seven minutes of interview on Dad's cassette tape recorder, and four pages of notes I had taken from the scrapbook, and it seemed as if that was only a sliver of what had to be done. There was also the fact that Mrs. Pease's reminiscences of old-time Vicinity didn't seem to fit together at all with the story of her work with animals. A lot of that had to do with cases in Lowell, Frontburg, and even New Hampshire, not with Vicinity at all.

Ms. Melander had spent time in class helping us think about the problems of doing oral history, such as people skipping from one decade to the next as they talked, or not remembering dates correctly, but I had a problem I suspected nobody else had: A lot of what Mrs. Pease said was about people she didn't like. Her older sister—the one whose legs I'd seen in the picture of Mrs. Pease as a child—had always been a sneak, according to her, and had ended by breaking into the house when Mrs. Pease was in the hospital (about five years ago, I gathered) and taking some antiques. Then there were various people who had been mean to their animals, and while most of them were dead, one was the Mrs. Robb who lived next door to Mrs. Pease. According to her, Mrs. Robb (or her grown son, who was in real estate) had once fixed the pipe from her own sump pump so it emptied into her (Mrs. Pease's) cellar, among other unneighborly gestures.

It was easy to see that Mrs. Pease's views on her neighbors weren't part of oral history, but what about the people she had taken to court over animal abuse? There were quite a lot of them, the scrapbook told me, and some had descendants still living in town who wouldn't be pleased to have the stories told again. Then there was the part about her last stay in the hospital. Mrs. Pease insisted several older ladies in town had used the excuse of "doing housework" for her to get into the house and "take things," including a Tiffany lamp. One of these same ladies had even, she hinted, been responsible for her fall in the first place. By now I didn't really believe all this, but it was going to be very hard to untangle her personal peeves from the story.

There was one good thing about the situation,

though, and that was that I was so busy wrestling with oral history that I easily wrote a boring little essay on "My Favorite World Leader of the Past" for Mr. Stropner. It took me less than five seconds to give up on doing the historical Count Dracula and settle for President Kennedy. I got a B on it, too.

When I answered the phone in the upstairs hall that night, I almost didn't recognize the voice, it was so thin and thready. "That you, Joan?" it asked. The time was after midnight, the cold carpet was gritty under my toes, and I had thought it would be my mom, saying they'd be home late from the Concord Band concert.

"Mrs. Pease?" I said. "Is that you?"

"I need some help," she said. "Cahn't seem to get myself up. C'n you come ovuh?"

CHAPTER 10

On the way to school the day after Mrs. Pease's accident, I had a list going round and round in my head: *Dottie, Daisy, and Dolly, the three D's. Midnight and Niggy are both black. And Mittens! She's black with white paws. That's six. Whitey, Goldie, and Lavender are named for their colors. That's nine. Mummy is the oldest, and then comes Dolly (but I counted her). Mummy makes ten. Pooky the tortoiseshell, and Willie the big gray one. Cuddles is the little brown tabby with six toes on her front feet. That's thirteen. But I know there's at least one more tabby besides Daisy and Cuddles. Oh, dear. What if one got out and I never noticed? And then there's Annie the dog . . .*

That first day I only worried about the animals. What would I feed them? I couldn't cook for them the way Mrs. Pease did, and some of them were fussy eaters, and very old. Mummy was twenty-one, and Dolly wasn't much younger. Goldie was still taking medicine to prevent his getting "blocked" again, and Whitey was always having colds. I knew because Mrs. Pease would send me to the store to get camphor to tie around his neck in a bag. It was the only cold remedy she had any faith in, and she got peeved with me when Boots showed up with sniffles and I wouldn't use camphor on him too.

Maybe I ought to call her vet, Dr. Finnegan. But I don't even know him! This is going to be too much for me!

By recess time I had definitely decided that someone else would have to take responsibility for the animals. I would feed them that night, but that would be that.

In the middle of lunch, I was paralyzed to hear the PA summoning me to the office. I thought of all the offenses I hadn't committed because I didn't have the nerve, and raced guiltily down the hall. The secretary's eyes were bright with interest as she said to me, "You have an urgent message to call this number at the hospital. You can use that phone." I wished the phone were at least in a booth so she wouldn't hear me, but the next period was due to start in four minutes and I had no time to find another.

A bored voice at the end of the line was not the hospital itself but a doctor's office. Would I be able to bring over a few things for Mrs. Pease? Oh, wasn't I a relative? Well, I was listed as next of kin. When was her birth date? What was her mother's maiden name? What did I mean I didn't know? And I couldn't come right over because I was in *school*? Well, really, these Medicare claims are enough trouble without—

Fortunately, the bell rang. I promised I'd do my best and hung up.

I went off to math class realizing that I still didn't know how Mrs. Pease was, or whether her hip was really broken.

When I got home from school, I called my parents at the store.

"Mother, what do they mean by 'things' for somebody in the hospital? I'm supposed to go over there."

" 'Things,' Jo? Oh, I guess just a nightgown, toothbrush, hairbrush, slippers, a good book . . ."

"A *nightgown*? Mom, do you have any idea what it's like over there? I probably couldn't find a nightgown, and if I did, I wouldn't be able to tell it from the dish towels."

"Did you look behind the door in the bathroom?"

After I had been silent for nearly a whole minute, Mom said, "Jo, hon, is something the matter?"

"Listen," I said, "when I think about it, I'm not sure there *is* a bathroom. Not one she uses. There's a bathroom upstairs but it's full of dust and boxes and things, and she hasn't been able to climb the stairs for years. And I've been all over the downstairs. There's just no place one could be."

"No bathroom!" Mom sounded as if she couldn't believe it. Then I heard Dad in the background. "It's possible, Lou. She probably uses the privy. A lot of the old houses still have them, mostly built-in because of the winter cold. I wonder what the Board of Health would think of that?"

"Well, tell Dad I'm not going looking for it," I said. "I guess I'll just see if I can find her bathrobe. And maybe some of her photographs. I've never seen her reading a book."

Boots and I felt, and maybe looked, like burglars as we climbed the creaky steps of the house on Oak Street in the dark of early evening and shone Dad's hooded flash lantern on the locks. There were two, one regular round one and one that looked like the kind on a trunk, with a hasp and padlock. That one stuck. I pushed and jiggled and blew on the key to warm it, the way Mother does when the car door lock is frozen, but nothing gave. I had put down my bag of groceries so I could thaw my hands in my pockets, when I felt Boots push up against me as if he were scared. He was looking at the big flat bird feeder that takes up almost one whole length of porch rail. There was something in it, not a bird. Something like a squirrel without the bushy tail. A pair of eyes shone red.

I must have moved, because the creature suddenly

leapt for the ground with a thud and scrambled under the porch. A few sunflower hulls pattered to the floor. Boots put his mittened hand into mine.

"Bad squoo?" he asked. Under the silky blond bangs, his eyes were worried.

"No, Bootsie, it wasn't a squirrel. I think it was a rat. The nerve of him, coming to a house with all these cats!" I made a joke, although there was a creepy feeling along the skin of my shoulders and neck. I had never seen a live rat before, but they made me think of bubonic plague and babies being bitten in slum kitchens.

The lock gave in at last, and Boots and I slipped into Mrs. Pease's front hall. It was very warm and very dark, in spite of the flashlight. The shadows at the top of the stairs were deep enough to hide anything or anybody, and behind the screen door to the kitchen, cats flickered and wavered like strange creatures underwater. I was prepared for Boots to be scared, but he only trotted cheerfully toward the kitchen door and I remembered he'd been wanting to play with "all those kitties" for months.

I heard a wooden sort of thump from the back of the house, which I told myself was just a shutter banging. But there wasn't any wind. Well, maybe it was a cat knocking something over. Boots was already working on the catch to the screen door, crooning, "Hullo, kitties." I opened the door for Boots, scooted him in ahead of me, and managed to block various cats with my legs until I got the door shut behind us. I pushed the light switch I remembered from last night and stood still under the bare bulb, just looking.

Last night I had been too excited and worried to look much at the kitchen. It had only been a dark place on the way to the animal room. Now I had a job to do, but I didn't know how to start. Boots was sitting on a little wooden stool, happily petting cats, but I couldn't even put down my paper bag full of cans. There was just no room.

The kitchen had a big sink in it, not white enamel but some sort of dark greenish-black stone. There was one metal tap over it, like one you would hook a garden hose to, and it was running a thin stream of water into the dirty pots and dishes in the sink. More used dishes covered the wooden drainboard, and there were white tracks on the board where the cats had walked in something sticky that had spilled from a dented enamel pot. The wall opposite me was taken up by two wooden tables of different heights, one greenish, one grayish. Their tops were covered with sheets of old newspaper, stained and shredded, and with cardboard cartons full of old rags, canned goods, food boxes, odd pieces of china, flashlight batteries, and who knows what else.

Through a dark door in the corner, I could see into a pantry with a battered little refrigerator and more cartons and shelves. In another corner was a built-in cabinet whose door hung open, showing nothing but medicine bottles, eyedroppers, fuzz-clogged cat brushes, bunches of papers, and boxes of pills. Behind me brooded the huge old stove like a black-and-silver hen, still giving out waves of heat and clucking to itself every once in a while as something shifted in its innards. The floor was bare boards that felt sticky underfoot. And in every corner were cardboard, plastic, or metal cat boxes filled with shredded newspaper and not easy to tell from the boxes on the top of the tables. The only clear place in the room was the big iron shelf attached to the stove, and I was afraid the bag would scorch if I put it there. I compromised on the seat of a straight chair that was padded with what looked like old pink nylon underwear.

Boots was sitting on the floor with Willie in his lap and Dolly climbing up his back. He had a smudge on his cheek that I knew was grape juice, and another on his hand that was red marker pen, but suddenly he looked very pink and scrubbed to me. I picked him up, gave him a hug, and carried him through the door into Mrs. Pease's bedroom, where I sat him in the big leather-seated rocker. "It isn't very neat in here, is it, Cowboy?" I asked him. "Why don't you just stay there with Willie and Dolly while I fix them some supper? You can see me right through the door."

I went back to the kitchen and decided I had to have somewhere to work, so I took two big cartons off one of the tables, dumped the junk from one into the other, and used the empty one for the dirty newspapers on the table. On second thought, I got the iron lid-lifter from its hook beside the stove, took off the stove lid, and stuffed the paper on top of the orange bed of coals. Sometimes fire seems very clean.

Next I checked under the furniture and in all the corners until I was sure I had a complete list of the animals, which I wrote on the side of the cat food bag: Annie plus Dolly, Daisy, Dottie, Mummy, Mittens, Midnight, Lavender, Whitey, Goldie (my Hobo), Niggy, Pooky, Willie, Cuddles, and (the one I had been forgetting before) Fiddle. (He's a big gray guy with a white chest.) Fourteen cats. And one overweight dog.

I looked around for some food dishes. There were plenty to be seen, but they were all caked with dried stew. I went into the dark pantry and poked around with the flashlight, looking for a light switch or some clean dishes, but I couldn't see anything except more cardboard cartons—one full of jars of jam, one with empty flowerpots, one with old newspapers, and one with a bunch of rusty spoons and forks. I decided the cats could eat their food out of the cans and congratulated myself that I had remembered to bring a can opener. Boots came in and wanted to help me, but he stopped after the first fight broke out. Before we had put down three cans, Whitey was growling at Midnight, Willie was beating up Mittens, and Cuddles, Dottie, and Daisy had started a sort of football scrimmage.

Goldie had backed into a corner growling at everyone, and the two young cats, Lavender and Pooky, were skulking around the edges and trying to snatch a bite whenever the food was left alone for a minute. I grabbed up the cans, swatted the cats that were still fighting, and announced, "Okay, Cowboy, we're going to have a roundup."

My idea was to leave the grabby cats in the kitchen and put the shyer ones in the bedroom. Old Mummy, in fact, had never moved from the daybed, and Niggy was hiding under the bureau. I put an empty carton over the open cans, and Boots and I started cat-herding. It must have been quite a sight: me and a three-year-old trying to divide fourteen hungry, unwilling, and nervous cats into two groups. Cats are slippery, of course, and elastic. Even when they don't use their claws (and some of them didn't), they have ways of sliding out of your hands that would surprise a snake.

Boots got scratched right away, and went back to the rocking chair with Pooky clasped suffocatingly tight to his red snowsuit. That left me to decide between muggers and victims. I picked Dolly, because she was old, Lavender, because he was little, Goldie, because he was still a stranger, and Cuddles, more because of her name than for any other reason, as the ones to join Mummy and Pooky in the bedroom. (Niggy had skittered into the pantry.) In the end, it was like playing soccer. I'd see a cat near the door, open it, and do a sort of dance, trying to get that one in and keep the others from oozing out. I was glad I had boots on, because both Daisy and Willie took swipes at me, though I think I ought to forgive Willie because I may have stepped on him. When I finally slammed the door behind Cuddles's fluffy tail, I was out of breath and I had a smarting place on my wrist where I had bumped into the hot stove. I was on the bedroom side of the door.

Boots's head was buried in Pooky's black-and-orange fur. "What's the matter, Cowboy?" I asked him.

One blue eye appeared from behind Pooky's ear. "Too noisy," he complained, and I realized I had been yelling things like "Darn you, get in there!" and "Oh, no, you don't!" for quite a long time.

"Sorry, pal. I got carried away."

This time, I put all the open cans down as far apart as possible and as quickly as possible. It worked pretty well, and I only had to break up one halfhearted fight. There certainly wasn't any problem with the cats' missing their regular food. They gobbled their Tuna Treat like lions pitching into zebra, all except Niggy, whom I couldn't coax out of the pantry, and Mummy, who still lay on Mrs. Pease's bed, twitching her thin, striped tail and watching the room through slitted eyes. Her coat, when I touched her, was dry and rough, and her backbone stood up like the teeth on a comb, but she licked some food off a spoon when I held it out for her and then made it clear that she didn't want any more.

I looked at my watch then, and saw that we'd been at Mrs. Pease's more than an hour. That was alarming. I had thought fifteen minutes would be enough to feed any number of cats. Until that moment, I had told myself that somebody else would have to take over—preferably a grown-up who didn't have evenings filled with homework. Now I began to realize that very, very few people would be willing to do this job. I looked around the kitchen, and the only word I could find for it was *filthy.* A couple of fat flies were hovering over the dirty dishes in the sink—in January. And there were places, under the sink and in corners, that my mind wanted to skip over although my eyes had seen them—places where the cats had not bothered with the cat boxes.

I thought then about the people I knew of in town who "did things" for people. There was sweet, gray-haired Mrs. Lisle, Ms. Melander's mother, with her weak heart. And there was energetic Mrs. Parker, who worked at the hospital and who, I knew, was a widow with four boys, the youngest in second grade. Aside from them, there were all the neighborhood ladies and mothers of people in my school. Lots of them baked brownies for the Vicinity Hockey League or the Girl Scout bake sale, brought hot casseroles to people when there was illness in the family, drove old people to the doctor, read aloud to hospitalized children, or raised funds to repair the town clock, plant trees on the Common, or pay the costs of kidney dialysis for retired town policemen. None of that sounded much like this job. I began to giggle as Boots and I hurried home, thinking of job advertisements I might write: *Wanted. Animal lover with no sense of smell. For unpaid job in unhealthy environment. Soccer experience helpful . . .*

Boots was tired, and I carried him the last block to my house, wondering how I was going handle the baby-sitting from now on. Obviously I couldn't keep taking him in there after he got curious and started to explore. He was still at the age where he put everything in his mouth.

When we got home, I washed our hands in Ajax Liquid and put peroxide on Boots's scratch. After his mother had called for him, I went upstairs and took a bath with some rose-scented bath oil (not manufactured by Uncle Charles).

CHAPTER 11

In the end, it was a very small package I put in my bike basket to take to the hospital the next morning, Saturday. I had found just a housecoat, some powder that said it was for dentures, an unopened box of candy from the windowsill by the bed, and the cigar box that held her favorite photos. I had looked all around for slippers, but couldn't find any except the terry-cloth ones that she held on with rubber bands. They had such big holes on the bottoms, I decided a nurse would just throw them out.

It was a mushy day, about thirty-five, with a grumpy wind and lots of puddles in the road for passing cars to splash at bicyclists. I went in the hospital door marked MAIN ENTRANCE VISITORS and froze when I realized I had no idea what I was supposed to do or where I was supposed to go. The lobby was full of Saturday visitors, customers in the gift shop, and people in white coats who looked as if they were on their way to save lives. Behind a desk saying INFORMATION was a cushiony woman in a pink smock. Beyond her were a long corridor, a pair of elevators, several doors saying things like RADIOLOGY and ADMISSIONS, and a wall covered with signs and arrows. I really didn't want to talk to the person in pink. Suppose it was the wrong time of day or I wasn't old enough to visit someone on my own?

The pink person was talking on the telephone and directing a father and a little boy to the cafeteria at the same time. She had pearl-colored fingernails so long that she had to dial the phone with a pencil, and the kind of shiny gold hair you usually see on the doll shelf in a toy store. I thought there was a good chance she wouldn't even see me if I went over and tried to get her attention. It was like the time I went into Jordan Marsh to buy a Christmas present for Mother and the store was closing before I could get anybody to take my money.

I stepped a little closer to a pillar beside the doorway, wondering whether Mrs. Pease would get the bag if I just wrote her name on it and left it there for the custodian to find.

"Well, hi, Jo. Doc Warnke's office told me you'd be in this morning. Come on, I'll take you up to Aggie's room." It was Mrs. Parker, with a badge pinned to her blouse and an armful of files with shiny metal covers. I hoped she hadn't seen me dithering around.

Mrs. Parker went to the desk, reached over it, and picked a large red plastic tag off a hook where it was hanging. It had a hole in the top, like a giant dog license. "Aggie's in three sixty-one," she explained as she bustled me off down the corridor. "That's third floor south. Just give the tag back when you leave."

I had no time to get ready to see Mrs. Pease. It was only about ten steps to her room from where the elevator let us off. In the bed near the door was someone I didn't recognize, and I looked toward the second bed, where a gray-haired woman with her foot in a cast was knitting a blue baby sweater. Mrs. Parker had gone to the head of the first bed. This was Mrs. Pease. She was lying on her back with her mouth open and her lips fluttering in and out like pieces of cloth. The rest of her face seemed flat and folded as an empty bag, except for the sharp bone of her nose. There was a tube in her nose, fastened with little pieces of pink tape, and another stuck in the bend of her elbow. Except for the flutter of her lips, she might have been dead.

I froze, but Mrs. Parker bent over her and patted her shoulder. "Come along, Agnes," she said. "Someone's here to see you." And to me: "You don't want to stay too long; she's still on medication. I'll come back for you in fifteen minutes." She whisked out the door as a voice said, quite loudly but hoarsely, "Who's thayuh?"

Clutching the paper bag tightly to my chest, I went and stood beside her. For a long moment we looked at each other. "So it's my Joan," she said with satisfaction. Her voice sounded strange because her false teeth were out and because of the tube. "What took yuh?" she said, teasing me, just as usual.

I said, "I had school yesterday. And I'm not allowed to ride my bike after dark . . . Look, I brought you some things from home."

She was very pleased to see the cigar box. She sorted through it with her good hand, taking out a snapshot of Annie when she was a puppy and a more recent one of herself on her porch with Willie and Daisy on her lap. Then she scrabbled for a minute and came up with a little rusty key with a curly handle. "Thayuh!" she exclaimed. "I knew 'twas in the box and not in my handbag. Now, Joan, you pull that cuhtain." She glanced meaningfully at the thing like a pale green shower curtain that separated the two beds. I pulled it down to the foot of the bed, not looking at the knitting woman in case she was offended at being shut out this way. Mrs. Pease took my hand and pressed the key into it. Lowering her voice, she said, "That's to my box, Joan. You'll need it."

I was confused, thinking of the cigar box I'd just

brought. "The box, the little trunk, at the foot of the daybed," she prompted. "In the animal room. It's got my paypuhs in it." She stopped talking and stared at the ceiling for such a long time, I began to think she'd forgotten I was there, except that she still had hold of my hand.

"Do you need some of your papers?" I asked after a while.

"Yes, paypuhs," she said, almost snappishly. "Don't rush me. Of cawse. It's those Medicayuh paypuhs. The nuhse wants 'em. All in a buff envelope. Says 'Medical' on it, or some such. You open my box and get them fuh me, all right?"

"Okay," I said. She let go of my hand and motioned me to put the cigar box by her pillow. "Now," she commanded, "tell me about my babies." I told her how they were eating well, how Pooky had cuddled on Boots's lap, and so on. "Mummy seems to miss you a lot. She won't get off your bed," I ended.

"Well, you just tell huh that Aggie's comin' home soon. She wuhn't be alone too long. Why, did you know, they fixed my old hip bettuh than new? That suhgeon, he come in an' told me that yestaday forenoon. Bettuh than new, an' all held togethuh with steel, that's what he said. Just a few days, now, just a few days . . . ."

Her voice trailed off, and I saw she had fallen asleep in the middle of her sentence.

"Don't worry about that, that's natural," said Mrs. Parker's voice from the doorway. "Aggie's got the constitution of a buffalo. Now come along to my office, I want to talk to you for a minute."

Mrs. Parker's office was small, cheerful, and cluttered with house plants and pictures of her kids. On her desk were two signs. One was black plastic and said, in white letters, CLARA O. PARKER, ASSISTANT ADMINISTRATOR. The other was painted on wood with yellow daisies. It said, THE HURRIEDER I IS, THE BEHINDER I GETS.

Mrs. Parker gave us each a mug of tea from an electric pot on top of her filing cabinet, and sat down. "Well, Jo, how did she seem to you?"

I was surprised. I'd thought she wanted to tell me something, not ask me. Still, I hesitated. I didn't want to say how awful Mrs. Pease had looked or how cold her hand had felt when she gave me the key to her "box." When I didn't answer right away, Mrs. Parker looked at me over the rim of her mug. "Well, how about it? Was she making sense?"

"Oh," I said, relieved. "Oh, yes. She made sense. She told me where to get her Medicare papers and asked how the animals were, and all."

Mrs. Parker seemed relieved, too, but for a different reason. "Fine. Wonderful. The nurses told me she wasn't talking much, and of course you never know when they're that age. It could be the medication, or it could not.

"So now, here's what I wanted to tell you. You ought to know, since you've been landed with the animals. Aggie came through the operation very well. I talked to her surgeon, that's Dr. DiMarco. A bad break, he said, high up in the hip, but it ought to heal up nicely. They'll keep her here for ten days or so, and then she'll have to go to a nursing home, certainly for two or three weeks. That means a lot of work for you, and something else: It's going to be expensive. Now, is there anyone who knows her finances—where her bank accounts are and so on? Someone will have to look after all that. And she must have checks coming in, social security and so on."

"I don't—I'm pretty sure she doesn't have a bank account," I said, remembering her mail. "When I buy groceries or medicine for her, she always gives me money from her purse."

"My Lord. No bank account, hunh?" Mrs. Parker shook her head. "Well, there are people who don't trust banks, you know. Especially those who lived through the Great Depression, like Aggie. Well, we'll just have to wait and see what comes in the mail. Who's getting it for her from the post office, by the way?"

"Oh, that's Mrs. Lisle. Her first name is Lily. She gets Mrs. Pease's mail and takes her to the hairdresser and the store sometimes too."

"Lily Lisle! Is she still around? She's no spring

chicken herself. Not but what she's a dear. Lily Lisle must be about the only person in town who puts up with Aggie. Except for you and me, of course, and we're young and strong. Well, I'll be in touch. Let me know if there's anything I can do for Aggie."

I was relieved that she was about to let me go. She talked so fast, and gave off so much energy as she did it, that I wanted to back away, as if I were standing in front of a furnace. As I opened her office door, I saw that a poster was taped to the inside of it. It showed a little old lady in an old-fashioned, crumpled black hat and granny glasses. Underneath, it said, "Pray for the dead, and fight like hell for the living. —Mother Jones, 1830–1930." I thought it was a gloomy thing to find in a hospital.

On the way home, I was worrying. Mrs. Parker was tough enough not to mind Mrs. Pease. Mrs. Lisle was too sweet to be bothered by her. But I wasn't like them. I had blundered into Mrs. Pease's web like a lazy fly with nothing better to do. Mrs. Parker thought I had been clever about getting Mrs. Pease into the hospital. She didn't know it was only because I had been scared to take the responsibility of lifting her. For that matter, Mrs. Pease thought I had been some kind of hero for catching Goldie. She had no idea that that big yellow pushover had actually caught me. So, as it turned out, I hadn't done anything much for anyone.

I decided to bike straight over to Mrs. Pease's with the trunk key. Those animals and that house were mine to look after, and would be for a long time if Mrs. Parker was right. All sorts of things could happen to them. What if they got sick? What if the pipes froze?

CHAPTER 12

THIS time, the animals seemed to know my step, or maybe they were just bored. So many furry bodies were pressed against the screen door, I could hardly tell one from another, and little Annie only barked as if she thought it was her duty.

The heat and the smell in the kitchen were really thick, maybe because I'd just come from the hospital, where the air-filtering system was so powerful, it hardly smelled of anything. The kitchen was the worst, and I knew I'd have to face up to cleaning those cat boxes soon.

Right now, however, I was in a hurry because my mother and I had a date to buy me a new spring jacket with some of my Boots-sitting money. I went straight into the animal room and brushed the soft drift of dust and cat hair off the top of the little trunk with a piece of newspaper. Kneeling in front of the trunk, I could see that it was made of ribbed wood and had once been covered with leather between the ribs. Generations of cats had taken care of that, though, and now there were only scabby little patches of brown on the wood. Both the key and the lock were rusty, but I was surprised when the trunk opened easily.

Inside, it was almost entirely filled with papers, loose and in bundles. I didn't see any buff envelope saying "Medical." This looked like being a long search. I started taking things out, one by one. The first buff envelope I came to had a bunch of electric bills in it, all carefully arranged in order, from 1956 to 1971, and stamped PAID. Next were some papers from insurance companies. There was an envelope marked "Old House" and another with "Social Security Administration" in one corner. The next one was unlabeled, so I looked inside. In it was a hundred-dollar bill.

I stared at it, wondering if it was real. I wasn't sure I had ever seen a bill that large before, but I didn't suppose she would save one that *wasn't* real. I put it back and went on looking. Next were a passbook for a savings account in Lowell (stamped CLOSED), and a fat folder labeled "Cemetary" in faded ink.

It was the old-fashioned, lacy-looking writing Mrs. Pease had had before she got her arthritis, and the spelling was hers too. I'd often heard her talk about the family plot in the Vicinity graveyard— "a nice shady place by a big maple." But this was a different kind of cemetery, as it turned out: an animal cemetery in New Hampshire. The envelope was stuffed with certificates showing Mrs. Pease had bought various plots, and there was even a sad little map marked with many printed squares and labeled, in handwriting that got shakier as the years went along, with names of animals I'd never met. Shorty, Spike, Blackie, Shep, Rosie, Baby Girl, and more. It made my eyes hot to read them. I put the map back carefully, and went on.

Cats rubbed up against me as I looked, humping their backs against my chin and parading their tails past my nose, and Annie came and lay with her gray muzzle on my knee. I found vets' receipts, blank forms for reporting animal abuse to the MSPCA, a collection of postcards with pictures of cute kittens, a little box with a child's flat gold locket in it. And then, on the bottom of the tray, there was a buff envelope saying "Medical." It was not very thick, and I remembered how Mrs. Pease distrusted doctors—all people doctors, and most animal doctors. Inside, the first thing I saw was a blue-and-white card saying "Medicare."

The phone rang, making me jump and drop Lavender, who had been trying to climb into the trunk. The phone was still on the floor by the window, where I had left it after I called the ambulance. I stared at it, thinking that I would be embarrassed if I answered it and had to explain what I was doing in Mrs. Pease's house alone. Four, then five, then six double rings, and I had just decided I ought to answer it when it startled me again by stopping. I put everything back carefully and locked the trunk, though not without lifting the tray to see what was underneath. There was nothing but more papers, however. I turned out the lights and wove my way through cats back to the kitchen.

I stood still in the doorway, just looking at the two long tables under the window opposite. I could remember exactly how I had cleared off a work space on one of them by putting two cardboard cartons on the floor.

The cartons were back on the table, just the way they had been.

But wait. Yesterday, I had emptied one out and put it over the open cans while I separated the muggers from the victims. I went over and looked at them carefully. One box was still filled with an assortment of old towels, crackers, baby food, and dusty Mason jars. The other one was empty. Had I really left them on the floor the way I thought? Or had I absentmindedly picked them up again? I couldn't be sure, but I hoped so. Otherwise, someone else had been in the house since Boots and I were there.

By the time I got home, the sky had gone from pewter to silver, with a bright spot in it where the sun was trying to shine its way through the tarnish. The wind had dropped, and it was even a little warmer, all of which was a good thing since I would probably have to bike over to the hospital again with the Medicare card. Or maybe Mother would take me.

As I went up the driveway I looked at our house, with its silly shingles and the tower on the corner, with its paint a little flaky and two upstairs shutters hanging crooked, like false eyelashes coming off. I had always wished our house was more like the other houses in Vicinity—tidy and unnoticeable or tidy and graceful. But compared with Mrs. Pease's house, ours wasn't a bit odd. *And* it had hot water and toilets and dishes you dared to eat out of. Not to mention some pretty nice people living in it. I went up the back steps feeling glad to be home.

The kitchen phone began ringing before I had the door shut. I picked it up and there was my mother, sounding anxious. "Johanna Justine Morse, where on earth were you? You can't have been at the hospital all this time, it's after lunch."

"I'm sorry. I had to go to Mrs. Pease's to look for some stuff."

"But I called there, several times. Don't tell me you didn't answer the phone . . ."

"You mean that was you?"

"Well, of course it was." She sounded cross.

"Now listen, Jo," she went on in a different tone of voice, "I'm not going to be able to leave the store this afternoon. I'm afraid we'll have to put off the jacket till next Saturday. Or maybe we can take Bootsie with us one day this week."

"Oh. Are you having a busy day?"

"Oh, pretty busy. On and off, you know. Bye-bye, sweetie, I'll see you later."

I could have bitten my tongue off the minute I heard myself ask if the store was busy. In the weeks since the Grand Opening, I had learned not to raise that topic. Dad still sounded cheerful when he talked about it, but he wasn't as good as he thought at hiding his worry. So I knew why Mother was trying to spend extra time there. A place never seems empty when there are two people in it.

I fixed myself some lunch, got back on my bike, and pedaled doggedly back to the hospital. When I got up to Mrs. Parker's office, she was on the phone, but she put her hand over the mouthpiece when she saw me come in. "Thanks a lot, kiddo. But you didn't have to bring it, you know. You could have just called me and given me the number."

I slouched away down the hall feeling grumpy and hoping I would never hear the word *telephone* again. Perhaps I would write a story about a brilliant scientist who discovers the radiation from telephones slowly drives you insane. The only thing is, she can't get anybody to pay attention to her discovery because they're all too busy talking to each other on the phone and nobody reads letters anymore. Or talks to people face-to-face.

I was all the way down in the lobby when I realized I was in the hospital and hadn't even gone to see Mrs. Pease. Part of me didn't want to go. I thought of the tubes and the way they had reminded me of worms. I thought of a face like a collapsed bag. But I made a detour to the gift shop.

I bought a card with a picture of three kittens in a pink basket, and wrote inside, *With Love from Annie, Mummy, Midnight, Mittens, Dottie, Daisy, Dolly, Lavender, Whitey, Goldie, Niggy, Willie, Pooky, Cuddles, and Fiddle. We miss you.*

Mrs. Pease, when I got there, was looking a lot better than she had that morning. She still had the tube in her arm, but her cheeks were pinker, her teeth were in, and someone had combed her hair so that it lay in neat, silky white curls. Also, somebody had arranged her photographs on the bedside table where she could see them. She took my card, and I handed her her glasses so she could read what was inside. "Those a' my babies," she said, ". . . my little family. You didn't miss a one." And suddenly, though she had looked for a minute as if she were going to cry, she gave me a mischievous smile. "They givin' you a hahd time ovuh suppuh?"

"Well," I admitted, "a little." I pulled up a gray metal hospital chair and sat on the cold green seat.

She looked at me sharply over the tops of her reading glasses. "You mustn't let 'em bamboozle you, you know. That Willie, he thinks he's cock o' the walk, and Fiddle's 'most as bad. Feed *them* fust an' it'll save you a lotta trouble." I nodded. "Then thayuh's Daisy. She and Whitey don't get along fuh sour apples. Maybe you'd bettuh put one of 'em in the othuh room."

"I did notice them growling at each other," I admitted, "but Mittens was chasing Lavender and they broke it up."

"Oh, that Mittens, she's a little devil! Always aftuh huh own way, even though she's just a baby. You got to watch afta Lavenduh when she's around. She'll steal his food quick's a wink."

"Don't worry, Aunt Aggie, he's getting his share. I put all the shy ones in the bedroom and all the pushy ones in the kitchen to eat."

Mrs. Pease laughed out loud. "An' how'd you manage *that*? With a a-tomic bomb?"

I was laughing too. "No, just some fancy footwork I learned in soccer. Boots and I had a real western rodeo."

"Well, I declare! That musta been quite a sight. Now, I just hiss at 'em, and sometimes I yell some or swat 'em with the broom and they mind pretty good, but then o' course they know me. And how is my little Bobby?"

"Oh, he's fine. He's really made friends with Pooky." I stopped because I didn't know what to say next. I was puzzled because Boots hadn't shown much reaction to his Aunt Aggie's accident. I might have made up a lie about him sending her a hug or something, but she had gone on to ask me about Mummy.

"I think she's all right, but I'm a little worried about her really. Every time I go, she's lying right on your bed. And she didn't even get down for her dinner. I had to give her some with a spoon."

"Well, after all, she and me're a bit old fuh dancin' jigs, ahn't we? I tell you what you do: Thayuh's some jahs of baby food on the kitchen table. You give huh some o' that in the spoon. If she wuhn't take that, then let huh lick it off yuh finguh. That'll bring huh right 'round." She stiffened against the pillow and turned so she could look me straight in the eye. Her voice had been getting thinner and thinner and I had leaned close, so I was startled when she exclaimed, "My land, what am I thinkin' of, child? You got to have some money for all this. Now you get me my handbag; it's in that drawuh." After I found the red plastic pocketbook, she had me open it for her. I was surprised not to see a wallet, only bits of paper, some keys, and some old envelopes. She sorted through it for a minute with her good hand and pulled out one of the envelopes, grayish and fuzzy at the edges. Her hand was shakier than I had seen it before, and instead of opening the envelope, she held it out to me. "That's fohty dollahs. You use it to buy food fuh my babies." She shut her eyes and took several breaths before she said, "You bettuh go now, Joan. I'm goin' tuh sleep."

I was halfway to the door when she added, without opening her eyes, "And get some ground beef for my Annie for a treat. Not too much, mind. It makes huh bilious."

"All right, Aunt Aggie, I will." Her lips were moving in and out as if she was already asleep, and I added, as much to myself as to her, "I'll take care of them all. I promise." I went home feeling better.

CHAPTER 13

DAD and Mother were home when I got there, but since nobody seemed to feel like talking, I decided to take care of the animals before the supermarket closed.

I put my bag of groceries down on Aunt Aggie's kitchen table and hunkered down on the floor to pat Goldie, who climbed right up on my knee and started rubbing his face on mine.

A loud thump sounded behind me. I jumped up and saw the pantry door opening slowly into darkness. To get to the hall, I'd have to go past that door; behind me was only the animal room, a dead end.

From the other side of the door came a scraping noise. Whoever was coming in wasn't in a hurry.

The sharp edge of the old stone sink was pushing

into my back. The door swung wider. Something dark and hunched over began coming toward me in jerks, with more scraping noises. Whoever was coming in was walking backward.

I had been good and scared, but now I was mad. "What are *you* doing here?" I demanded loudly.

"Aaaaagh!" The person in the dark duffel coat gave a terrified leap and vanished into the pantry, leaving a large metal garbage can in the doorway. I could hear fumbling noises, as if someone was trying to get out the door to the woodshed. Suddenly I was brave. I charged into the pantry and jerked on the light. The duffel coat belonged to a big boy who was cowering back against the wall as if I had two-inch fangs, a thick mane, and a loud roar. I just stood looking at him because it seemed that anything else I did would scare him even worse.

He was tall enough to be sixteen or seventeen, but his round face looked younger, with thick, curly blond hair, blue eyes, and a cleft chin. Under the coat, I could see an ugly argyle-knit sweater in red, gray, and blue over too-big polyester slacks with maroon checks. They were not the sort of clothes for a kid, I thought. There was a prickle of blond beard on his jaw too. Maybe, then, he was not a kid. But his eyes still looked like Boots's after we'd seen the rat, so I tried to sound friendly when I said, "Hullo. What's your name?"

He relaxed a little, but he didn't say anything or stop watching my face to see which way I was going to jump. I turned my back on him and took a step toward the kitchen.

"I came to feed Aunt Aggie's animals," I said over my shoulder. "I'd better do it; they're hungry." I made myself very busy, giving Annie her hamburger first, then setting out rows of cans and beginning to separate muggers from victims.

A voice from the pantry doorway said, "Aunt Aggie's sick." He was standing watching me, not frightened now but interested, and something in the way he spoke made me think. Kids in school joked about being retarded, but not with me. I felt a little too weird myself to joke about anyone else. I would have been afraid of him, I supposed, if I had known beforehand. "Yes," I answered, picking short words, "she hurt her hip. She's in the hospital."

He edged farther into the kitchen, pulling the trash can after him. "Billy's gonna clean up, okay?"

"Is that your name—Billy?"

"Yup."

He began picking up the cat boxes one by one and dumping them into the trash can. It was smelly, but it didn't take long. Then he got a newspaper off the pile of *Lowell Suns* in the pantry, knelt down on the floor, and began shredding it a few pages at a time. He worked carefully, tearing good, even strips, and puckering his forehead in concentration. Before he hauled the trash out, I threw in the empty cat food cans from last night. I had been worrying vaguely about what to do with the garbage.

When Billy came back in, he had a big, old-fashioned scuttle of coal in one hand. He set it down in front of the stove, opened a bulging black door in the stove's front, and began shoveling old ashes into an empty coal scuttle that was standing beside it. The cats were all eating, and I watched him as he rattled a heavy grate back and forth, opened a little sliding vent on the side, turned the damper in the big black chimney, and shoveled more coal in through the top. It struck me that Billy might not talk like other people, but he obviously knew exactly how that old stove behaved.

I certainly hadn't been very observant. How could I have supposed any stove would burn right through Thursday night, all day Friday, and on into Saturday without someone to take care of it? Obviously, Billy had been coming in regularly, and he must have been the one who moved the cartons. In fact, he must come every day to take care of the stove. Aunt Aggie couldn't possibly carry that heavy scuttle.

When he was through with the stove, he picked up Dolly. Dolly was a plain, no-nonsense cat, white spotted black, but she treated Billy as if he dressed in catnip and bathed in cream, while he rubbed her stomach and called her Dolly-puss. Watching them, I remembered that Dolly was the granddaughter of Snowball, whom Aunt Aggie had given to—what was her name? "Goodson," I said. "You must be Mrs. Goodson's son Billy."

He looked at me between Dolly's ears. "Momma? You know my momma?" He was beaming. I guessed I'd just mentioned his favorite person in the world.

"No, I don't know your mama, Billy, but maybe I'll meet her someday."

He nodded. "My momma's nice." He reached out to put Dolly on a table, and I saw that his hands were big and strong like a man's, with some golden hair on the backs, but the nails on his stubby fingers were chewed like a nervous child's. Apparently being Billy Goodson had its worries and problems too. However, as I watched him get ready to go, I was feeling hopeful about the weeks ahead. With Billy to help out with the stove and the trash, my job didn't seem so impossible.

I went back in the animal room and gave Mummy her baby food. This time, she let me pet her while she licked the spoon. While I was doing that, I absentmindedly picked a flea off my sweater. That made me stop still. Even Watermelon gets a few fleas in the summer, but I'd never heard of fleas in the winter. Then I thought about the flies in the kitchen. It was one more reason not to bring Boots with me again.

Over the next week or so, I spent quite a lot of time in Aunt Aggie's parlor, going over her book and photographs for my project. I wanted to know exactly how many animals she had found homes for over the years, but it wasn't easy. Was the "black kitten" she had placed with a family named Watberger on June 10, 1939, one of the "Three Orphan Kittens Found in Cellar" with whom she'd had her picture taken by the *Frontburg Advertiser* in April? And what about the "rabbits to Tom Hart" mentioned in 1966? I supposed this must be the same Mr. Hart who had a sign saying HARTS RABIT'S FOR PET & SHOW in front of a house on Lowell Road, but did the note mean two rabbits or twenty or a truckload? Still, Ms. Melander said she was pleased with the notes I showed her.

I began to get interested in the projects the other kids in the group were doing. One of them was Jenny Carson, who was interviewing her ninety-four-year-old great-grandmother, who still lived where she had been born, in the Carson Homestead on Carson Road. There were also stuck-up Lucinda Cray, who carried on a lot about how she was descended from Ralph Waldo Emerson; a short boy named Dan, who was writing up the history of gravel removal; and a few others who hadn't really got going yet. The best project belonged to Jason Drutch, a jock type from another class, whom I'd seen a couple of times at the bookstore.

Jason had found some old family papers that seemed to contain a clue to the location of a whole lot of the town's oldest gravestones, which were supposed to have been lost when the burying ground was moved to a new location in 1732. The papers said the stones had been dumped in the woods somewhere near Storrow's Pond, and Jason was all hot to go prospecting for them, except that the ground was under two feet of snow. The old slate gravestones from around here have weird and wonderful carvings on them—death's hands, angels, weeping willow trees, and verses. I thought it would be exciting to find those missing stones, although it's not my ancestors who would have been buried under them, since Dad's family only moved here in the 1860s and Mom's from Worcester. I might have been envious if I hadn't been so involved with Aunt Aggie and her animals.

I went to see Aunt Aggie as often as I could after school, although sometimes she was grumpy about it when I missed a day or two. Mostly, Mother would drive me when she got home from work. She still had her part-time bookkeeping job in Frontburg, and I noticed she and Dad had stopped talking about her giving it up. Instead of letting me tell Mrs. Vesey I would have to bring Boots home earlier, Mother had said she would take him herself. "I know you need the money, Jo" was all she said about it. Boots was perfectly happy to go shopping with her while I visited Aunt Aggie. I did take him with me once, but he hung back and seemed so shy and tongue-tied that Aunt Aggie's feelings were hurt and I didn't try again.

Each time I went now, I'd help her sort through her mail. I was surprised, after a few days, at the number of get-well cards that came, from places as far away as Methuen, Worcester, and even New Hampshire. It seemed that word of her accident was "getting around" and a lot of people remembered the lady who'd given them their dog or cat. Mostly they just said "Best Wishes" and signed a name I didn't know. Several people signed their animals' names as well. But one card was so remarkable that I wondered if I was getting the handwriting right as I read it to her. It came from Sudbury and had a big bunch of purple flowers on the front. " 'Dear Agnes,' " I began, and then stopped at the next word. " 'Sport, Spr–, Spirit.' Can that be right—'Spirit'?"

"That's right, Joan, that's right. My friend Mitzi, she has a Spirit Guide." From her tone, it seemed Aunt Aggie thought that explained everything.

"Okay, then: 'Spirit came to me last Thursday said it was a bad time for you. How I wish I had called, I know I could have prevented but you know my situation. She was much upset said it was your bad aspect. We have been working for you every night now hope you feel the Influnce. All the Angel Band be with you in prayers and in comunion. Spirit says worst is over you will recieve good news by letter. Beware of a dark man he does not have your wellfare at heart.

When life's darkest hour is on us,
When we need a helping hand,
Heaven shines its Light upon us,
Spirit helps us understand.

If you need more just call. You know how.' "

Aunt Aggie was so quiet when I finished, I thought she might be going to go into a trance or something and "call" her friend Mitzi right then. However, she soon came back to earth and said in her normal voice, "Well, wasn't that kind?" just as if Mitzi had sent her a potted plant. "I knew my accident would get through to huh," she confided. "Mitzi has the Gift."

I had thought nothing much about Aunt Aggie could surprise me anymore, but I knew better than to ask too many questions. Aunt Aggie didn't like people being curious about her affairs. However, the idea that she was friends with a medium made sense to me now. She often talked about dead people, such as her mother, and even her former animals, as if she had heard from them recently. I suspected now that she wasn't just being forgetful.

The rest of the mail that day was routine, but it gave me a chance to bring up something that had been worrying me. At first she had seemed too weak to deal with it, but now she was stronger, even standing up every day with the help of two nurses. I'd noticed, too, that she had the energy to complain —about the food, about not going home yet, and about the snoring of the patient in the other bed.

"Aunt Aggie, what are we going to do about these bills? And the social security check," I added, remembering how she had fretted for the last two days in case it was lost in the mail. Apparently I had picked the right time.

"Money odduhs, that's what I do when I can't get 'round myself. You buy 'em at the post office and mail 'em. Only mind you keep the receipts. That phone company is just plain *mean.*"

"What about the check?"

"Oh, the bank'll cash that. They know me. Heyuh, give it to me and I'll sign it."

But when I gave her the check, her lunch tray to write on, and her ballpoint pen with "The Friends of Animals" on it, we discovered something. Since the accident, the shaking of her hand had gotten much worse. She tried it first alone, then holding it with her other hand and me holding the tray. There were spots of red high up on her cheeks, and two white marks by the sides of her nose when she finished, but nothing legible on the check back. "I got to sign things," she said. Her voice was high with something like panic. "I got to sign things. When you can't sign things, they call in the lawyuhs and then they come an' take you away." She was breathing hard now, and the shaking had spread from her hands to her whole body. "Come sit by me, Joan, and steady my hand. I can do it if you steady me."

Sitting beside her on the hospital bed was not only awkward, it was against hospital regulations, but I slid down carefully, not to jounce the broken hip, and put my hand around her thin one. There was so little flesh on it that the hand and the wrist were the same width until they got to the swollen knuckles. My left arm seemed to be in the way, so I put it around her shoulders. But though I tried to guide her stiff fingers, the result was no better than before. In a minute I felt her wince, and realized I had squeezed too tight.

I let go, and saw tears in her eyes, of pain or frustration. For a minute, she seemed to have forgotten I was here. The woman in the other bed had fallen asleep (not snoring) over her knitting, and nothing could be heard but someone's television, far down the hall. Without asking, I picked up the red pocketbook from the bedside table and opened it. Inside, I knew, was her social security card, signed *Agnes C. Pease* in shaky but legible writing. I put it down on the lunch tray and studied it: the old-fashioned script *s* with the little loop at the top, the bigger loop that began the capital *C,* the way the capital *P* was joined to the *e.* Thoughtful, I picked up the pen and tensed the muscles in my hand until it trembled. *Agnes C. Pease,* I wrote on the clean paper doily that stuck out from under the used plate. *Agnes C. Pease.* Aunt Aggie was watching me now. I saw that I had slanted the letters too much forward and did it again.

This time it looked right. I smiled at her—a little, questioning smile—and she smiled back with that mischievous sparkle I loved, eyes dancing and lips puckered in mock disapproval. Without a word, I picked up the pen and signed her name to the back of the check. Without a word, she nodded. "I'll call the bank laytuh an' tell 'em you-uh comin' " was all she said. "They can't keep *us* down. No *suh*!"

CHAPTER 14

AFTER Aunt Aggie had been in the hospital a week or so, everybody in town seemed to know, about not only the accident, but who had called the ambulance and what brand of cat food I was buying for the animals.

Lots of afternoons Boots and I would go downtown with his sled so I could buy animal food, pay bills, or drop by the bank.

Two women in cloth coats and plastic rain bonnets stopped me one day to say, "What a shame," and compliment me on "taking care of dear Agnes's animals." One was stout and gushy and told me there weren't enough young people who understood the spirit of charity. The other was thin and timid. She pressed my hand as they were leaving and whispered, "*She* wouldn't do what you're doing. Not in a million years." It was only when she turned away that I saw from her profile they had to be sisters.

I went into Jamus's Hardware one afternoon for some nails to fix Aunt Aggie's porch light, which had come loose in a windstorm. Everybody in town knows Mr. Jamus because in addition to owning the hardware store, he's the chairman of the finance committee, operates a maple syrup business, and is the town's tree warden. He has a face like a baked ham—big, browned, and shiny. Even the thick glasses' frames he wears remind me of pineapple rings, and his voice is almost as loud as his laugh.

"Well, well! You still running errands for that old grouch from Oak Street? She's the only soul in town meaner'n I am. That's what the wife says, and she ought to know, ha-ha! Nails? You don't want nails for a job like that! Tell you what, young lady. You just leave this to me. I'll stop by an' take care of it on m' way home, all right? No, don't thank me till I do sump'n for ya. An' you tell that cantankerous old biddy to hurry up 'n get well, you heah? Place ain't the same 'thout her raising, hmph, *Hades,* ha-ha!"

Mr. Jamus had always made me nervous with his jokes and his loudness, but I thought I owed it to Aunt Aggie to say something. "I'll tell her to get better or else you'll win the Cantankerous Contest, okay?" Everybody in the store laughed, including Mr. Jamus.

That evening when I arrived to feed the animals, the porch light was hanging straight again, fastened by four bright new screws, and there was a ten-pound bag of dry cat food leaning against the porch rail.

Another afternoon, Officer Savineau pulled up beside me and Boots in his patrol car, making it a big day for Boots. He said he'd been wanting to tell me not to worry about the house. The boys had an eye on it, he said, in case anyone tried to break in. "There's always rumors," he explained to me. "Folks'll say all kinds of things. She got any valuables in there?"

"Not unless you have a cat museum," I said. But his question set me thinking, and after he'd obligingly flashed his lights for Boots and showed him the button that made the siren go, I took us straight back to the house on Oak Street. I still didn't want Boots running around in the animal room, but that wasn't where I was going. Anything valuable would be in the parlor or the dining room.

When we got there, Boots had a joyful reunion with Thunder while I walked around opening drawers and poking into closets where I really had no business. However, the only reward for my nosiness was more uncertainty. There was no silver in the dining room drawers, but what about the tall cut-glass vase that sparkled like winter icicles when the sun struck it? And the painted dishes in the china cupboard? I had seen some like them in an antique store window recently. And my friend Julie's mother collected Victorian furniture and had a marble-topped table with scalloped edges and a spindle-back rocker just like the ones in Aunt Aggie's parlor.

Several pieces of furniture had little notes taped to them. On one, I noticed the message *For my dear friend Mrs. Beatrice Langley* had been angrily crossed out.

I was getting ready to feed the animals and go, when I remembered something. Aunt Aggie had another source of income besides her social security (three hundred thirty-eight dollars and eighteen cents a month), I had learned. For years, she had saved from the money she made by renting rooms and working in the gardens at the Squanatisset Inn, and with her savings she had bought some stocks that now paid her small amounts of dividends. Even though Dad and Mother were amazed at how little money Aunt Aggie had to live on, cashing checks for forty or sixty or three hundred thirty-eight dollars made me feel as if I had a lot of money to lose. I had cash of hers in my pocket now, but the stocks themselves were in the little trunk in the animal room. Aunt Aggie had told me so: "It's whayuh I keep my paypuhs. No bank deposit fuh me. I want 'em unduh my eye." And stock certificates were certainly "valuables." Grandpa Morse had left me five shares of some kind of steel, and they were in our bank along with Dad's army discharge, their wedding certificate, and Mother's star sapphire ring that she only wore on her birthday and New Year's Eve.

I went into the animal room and dragged the little trunk after me into the parlor. Then I got Pooky for Boots to play with and opened the trunk with the little brown key. Inside were the bundles of papers I remembered, but nothing as big as Grandpa Morse's steel shares. I lifted out the top tray and saw more papers in the bottom, plus three cigar boxes like the one she kept her mementos in. Hoping they had more photos for my project, I lifted them out, but as soon as I did, I knew I was wrong. They were heavy.

Sitting there on Aunt Aggie's hearth rug, with its hooked pattern of flowers, leaves, and a big brown deer, I began opening those three boxes. They contained jewelry, an incredible jumble of jewelry. I'm no better at jewelry than I am at antiques, but some of this had to be real—not rubies and emeralds, but a heavy gold locket and chain, a big gold man's pocket watch with *J. Cully* engraved on the back, a gold brooch with a sort of fringe of irregularly shaped pearls, and a set of earrings that had to be garnets, clear and red as the little seed capsules inside a pomegranate. There were some cameos too—those portraits that look like Greeks and Romans carved into polished pink shell—and a gold bracelet set with golden-brown stones that I thought might be topazes.

Mixed in were other things that I could tell were junk: a cheap pin in the shape of a kitten with red glass eyes, three strands of fake blue pearls, and a pin in the shape of a pink plastic flower like the kind that comes on the top of a birthday cake. Right at the end I found a little hinged maroon leather box that had three rings in it. One was tiny, a child's ring with a little pearl; one was silver (or platinum?) and set with what I was somehow sure was a real diamond, plain and square. The last had a star sapphire between two leaves with tiny diamonds on them. It was as big as the one my mother had, and the star in the blue stone shone misty silver, like the moon on a cold autumn night.

After that, it was no big thrill to find the stock certificates flat against the bottom of the box. I put everything back the way it had been, retrieving a gold chain and the blue pearls (with which Boots had decorated Thunder's bridle) and locked the box. Then, after a moment's thought, I hid it upstairs in the bathroom, figuring it was the last place somebody would expect to find valuables.

That evening, while I was grating cheese in our kitchen, I asked my mother about stock certificates and also about star sapphires. "Well, *of course* they're valuable, sweetie. Since the stocks are still paying dividends, they must be active, and they certainly shouldn't be sitting where they could be burned in a fire, let alone stolen. You'll really *have to* persuade Mrs. P. to get a safe-deposit. And a checking account too. Do you realize how much time you're spending traipsing back and forth to the bank and the post office? (Dump these noodles in that boiling water, will you?) And you might mention to her that it costs fifty cents every time you buy a money order, but the bank only charges ten cents for a check *and* you earn interest."

Dad came in from the living room, where he'd been watching the news. He looked tired, but he ran his hand over my hair and said, "What's the news with Aunt Aggie?" Still I felt a tiny fear nipping at my stomach because I could tell from his tone of voice that he had stopped listening before I began to tell him.

The next day, on the way to the local history group, I bumped into Lucinda Cray, who had stopped in the hall to rearrange her waved, curled, and moussed chestnut hair. Before I could apologize, she said in her sweet, high voice, "I suppose all this attention has gone to your head."

"What attention?" I said, feeling stupid. Lucinda only laughed. "You are *too much,*" she said, in such a tone of voice that I was really glad to see Jenny Carson arriving so we could go into the classroom together.

"What has the Crayfish got her claws into *you* for?" she whispered, and added, "That's what I call her—she nips you when, and where, you least expect it." The fact that we both went into the room giggling probably didn't make Lucinda like me one bit better.

Later that day I found out what Lucinda had meant, more or less. I was eating my lunch in my usual inconspicuous way, down at the bottom end of a table whose top end was occupied by four noisy seniors, when two boys dumped their trays down beside me. One of them was Jason Drutch, and one was a kid I hardly knew, named Phil something.

"Say, Jo," he began, "Jase says you're caretaking the haunted house. Is it real creepy in there?"

"Creepy?" I knew what he meant, but I was sizing him up. Was he the type who would try to break in for thrills, or was he just curious?

"Yeah, creepy. Man, when I was a kid I'd have died rather than even pass that place. Used to go all the way around by Wiggins Street to avoid it after school. Of course, it's different now. But that old lady—Mrs. Pease—she yelled at us once, and I swear she was carrying a broom. One Halloween a bunch of us dared each other to ring her bell. We were about nine, I guess. We never even got up the front walk. There's this red glow in her hall. Like blood, you know what I mean?" He laughed, and I decided he was okay and I wouldn't have to scare him away.

I said, "She uses the broom to get around with. Instead of a cane, that's all, because her arthritis hurts. I've never heard her mutter even one tiny spell."

"But she steals cats," said Jason. "At least that's what Joey Norman said. The Jardines—used to live on Oak Street—she found their cat in her yard, shut it up, and said it was hers. Never did give it back."

I was about to cast doubt on this story when I remembered the trouble over Frosty. "Okay," I admitted, "she may be a little extreme about animals sometimes, but she's certainly no witch, and there isn't one scary thing in her house." I didn't know how wrong I was.

"Well, you just be careful anyway," said Phil seriously. "My mom knows the Langleys. Mrs. Langley and some other ladies, they were helping Mrs. Pease the first time she fell down, about ten years ago. You know, walking the dogs and things. And when she came home, didn't she just start accusing them of stealing her stuff? As if Mrs. Langley'd be the kind to take things. Her husband used to be the rector of our church! My mom says she hopes you haven't bit off more than you can chew."

"Aw, come on, Phil!" exclaimed Jason. Could it be that he didn't want my feelings hurt? I felt my face grow warm and took a big bite of pizza to hide it.

"It's okay," I said. "Do you think I don't know she gets into feuds? She doesn't have much of anybody left to count on, that's all. I wouldn't," I added, remembering the smell in the kitchen, "have gotten myself into this if there were anyone else to do it."

"Well, anyway," said Jason, helping me change the subject, "it still must be kinda weird for you, creaking around in that empty house with nothing but two hundred cats. You're sure there isn't a ghost, hunh?"

I laughed to show them I was joking. "Oh, yes, there's a ghost," I said, thinking of Billy, "but I've already met him and he's harmless."

CHAPTER 15

I meant to talk to Aunt Aggie about her valuables the next time I saw her, but when I got to the hospital, she was having a fight with two doctors, a nurse, and Mrs. Parker.

You sometimes see a cat who's backed into a corner, holding off three or four dogs. That's what Aunt Aggie looked like, a scrawny but determined white cat, settled back on its haunches and batting at anything that dared come within range. Her eyes were as sharp as needles, and you could almost see the tip of her tail twitch in triumph as she announced, "Home is whayuh I'm goin', and none o' *you* goin' ta stop me, neithuh."

Three of the four big, healthy people standing around her looked as frustrated and bewildered as if they'd been curious dogs who'd got their noses scratched. Only Mrs. Parker seemed relaxed. She was standing off to one side with her arms folded across the front of her green cardigan. She looked as if she was trying not to laugh.

"—only want what's best for you, Agnes," the big, dark-haired doctor was saying. "Why, I'd be risking my professional reputation if I let you go home before you could take care of yourself. What would you do, all alone in your room at night?"

"I'm all alone in the daytime too," snapped Aunt Aggie. "I'll just *manage,* like I always do."

"But Sunnydale is really such a friendly place," protested the younger, shorter doctor. He had thin blond hair and eyebrows so pale they were almost white. "I'm sure you'd find lots of friends there."

Mrs. Parker caught sight of me and drew me out into the hall. "Look here, Jo," she said, "it's funny, but it's not funny either. Why, she can't get into or out of bed by herself yet, or sit on the johnny. The thing is, the Medicare regulations won't let us keep her here beyond next Monday. Now, no nursing home is a palace, but Sunnydale's clean and it's accredited, and it's in Vicinity, where people can come see her easily. They even have a visiting physiotherapist, which is what she needs. If I get them all out of the room, do you think you can do anything with her?"

I wanted to say, "Who, me?" but I shut my teeth tight and thought.

"If she goes home now," I said, "she's still going to have all sorts of *people* coming to the house—this physio-whatsy-ist, and that doctor and so on, right?" Mrs. Parker nodded.

"She wouldn't like that," I said. "They'd find out—things."

Mrs. Parker narrowed her eyes. "I see what you mean. Whereas later . . ." She became her usual brisk self. "Give me five minutes to get that room empty." She had it cleared out in one. I think they were glad to go.

When I walked in, Aunt Aggie looked a little tired, but more than a little smug.

"I heard some of what those doctors were saying," I told her.

"Well? Was I wrong?"

"I think—I think maybe there are some things you haven't thought of." I told her about all the people coming to the house.

"Hmph," she said, not too angrily. "I thought you'd be glad not to have to feed the animals anymore."

"But I *would* have to. Don't you see? And I'd have to cook for *you,* too, or somebody would. You need both hands to hold on to that walker." I didn't need to mention the shaking that had led me to sign the checks for her.

"The laaahst time this happened to me, some veddy nice laadies brought me my meals on a traay." She drew out her words in a parody of a polite Boston accent.

I hated to spoil her fun, but I had to. "I know they did, you told me all about it. And you didn't eat one bite. You said that food was too spicy for you. Besides," I added, "that was Mrs. Langley and the church auxiliary. You say you're not speaking to her anymore."

Abruptly she leaned forward and peered at me, not so much like a cat now as like an old turtle from the safety of its shell. "I'm goin' to hafta go to that place, ain't I, Joan?"

"I guess so," I said, and wondered why I felt like a traitor. "They said it's only for a few weeks."

I left, after telling Mrs. Parker that Mrs. Pease had agreed to go to the nursing home, and getting my hand shaken by the head nurse.

The day after that, there was one cat missing at feeding time. Mummy had come down off the bed some days before, but I still gave her baby food in my lap since she wouldn't touch the canned stuff. That should have left thirteen, though, and I was standing with the thirteenth can in my hand. Automatically I started down the now familiar list: Daisy, Dottie, Dolly, Mummy, Mittens, Midnight, Goldie, Lavender, Whitey . . . Where was Lavender? He should have been in the bedroom with the other "victims." Most of the cats had very quickly learned which room they were going to be fed in;

there were only a couple of troublemakers, such as the ever hungry Daisy.

Lavender was in the bedroom, I found, but not eating. He was lying on his side under the bed, and he had been vomiting. Dr. Finnegan's number was still on the side of the phone. I dialed it without even thinking that it was after five o'clock, but either I was lucky or Mitzi's Spirit was watching out for Aunt Aggie's animals. Dr. Finnegan could give me an emergency appointment.

The next number I dialed was my own. Would Mom be home from work and willing to drive me to the vet's? She still had reservations about Aunt Aggie, and I could imagine her insisting on Dr. Kantor because he was closer. However, she was still a softie. It wasn't more than half an hour before we got to the clinic, with Lavender huddled in my lap on some not very clean towels from a box in the pantry. His eyes were open now, but I could hear his breath rattling even over the engine of our old yellow Honda, and when I patted his cream-colored sides he didn't so much as twitch his tail tip. Mother stopped me under the streetlamp outside the clinic and I felt Kleenex scrape my face. I hadn't realized till that minute that I was crying.

The big young man behind the desk inside was very nice to us. He took us straight in past all the barking dogs and crouching cats, and put Lavender carefully on the shiny steel examining table in a room where Dr. Finnegan was already washing his hands. He was a friendly-looking man, about my parents' age, with a brown mustache that stuck out like a snowplow blade, thick brown hair, and large square hands. He listened to Lavender with a stethoscope, took his temperature, and looked inside his mouth. Lavender seemed so little and helpless with his eyes shut and his paws hanging loose. Dr. Finnegan finished his examination and said to me, "Okay . . . Joanne, is it?"

"Oh. Johanna. With an *h*."

"Okay. Look here, I'm afraid Mrs. Pease has a pretty sick cat. I can't be sure until I do a test, but it's likely Lavender has something called feline parvovirus, and if so, he won't get over it. Parvo is contracted by prolonged intimate contact. In young cats like this it often comes from the mother's milk since it takes a few months to develop. I'm very sorry indeed, but once they have it, there's not much anyone can do. I know Agnes will take it hard too. I heard she's in the hospital."

"She broke her hip," said my mother. "Johanna's the one who called the ambulance, and she's been coping ever since." I was surprised to hear a note of pride in her voice.

"You don't say! You've taken on quite a job there, young lady. Now let me tell you something: You mustn't feel that there was anything you could have done to prevent Lavender from getting sick. If it's parvo, he caught it long before he came to Mrs. Pease's and he'd have got it just the same, whether she was home or not. You needn't worry about the other cats either. It usually only passes between littermates or mothers and kittens. How are the others? Eating well?" I nodded. "Well, then, you go on home. We'll do what we can for him, and you call in the morning and see what's happened." He let us out a side door, and we went around to the car without speaking.

In the morning the young man at the clinic told me very regretfully that Lavender the Siamese was dead. "It goes to their lungs," he explained. "The little guy had pneumonia."

"I see," I said. "Um. Thanks a lot."

"By the way," he went on, "Doc said to tell you he'll take care of the body. I mean about the *arrangements.*"

"What arrangements?"

"Mrs. Pease, she always has special arrangements for her animals that die. She'll tell you herself. Look, Doc said to call anytime if you have problems."

All day long I dreaded having to tell Aunt Aggie about Lavender. By the time I got to the hospital, I still didn't know what I was going to say.

Aunt Aggie said it for me, as soon as she saw me: "Come in and tell me about my little Lavenduh." I hope I didn't look as guilty as I felt. "How did you find out?" I blurted out.

"Dr. Finnegan come to see me. Lunchtime. Seemed to think you was blamin' yuhself, but I tell you what I told him, an' we both know it's true: that FPV is bad stuff. Like rabies. Once they got it, they don't get bettuh. 'Twas just God's will. Now tell me how you found him."

I told her, although it made us both cry. In the end, she blew her nose, wiped her eyes on the bed sheet, and said matter-of-factly, "Dr. Finnegan's put him on ice fuh me. Till I'm ready fuh my arrangements."

"On ice?"

"Oh, yes," she said, misunderstanding my surprise, "they got a big freezuh. Fuh serums and samples and things. Now, when you see Billy, you tell him to get anothuh box ready. He knows how to do that, all right, even if he is a bit wantin'. Tell him to ask his mama for some creosote if he's out, and I'll pay her. Then when I get home, we'll take care of him, Billy and I. We done it many times befowuh."

"All right," I said, not understanding very well, and trying to remember what creosote was. I supposed all this had to do with those lots she owned in the animal cemetery.

Then came a couple of days when I was busy helping get things ready for Aunt Aggie to go to the nursing home. It seemed she couldn't just arrive there. Forms had to be filled out, and I had to write the answers for her. That was how I found out that she was not seventy-three, as she sometimes declared, or even "over eighty," as she'd said on the form for the telephone company, but eighty-eight years old. No wonder, I thought, that she'd gotten over Lavender's death sooner than I expected. How many generations of cats had lived and died in her house? And then I remembered that one day I would be alive without Watermelon, without even my parents. The thought made me shiver, and then I was back in the overheated hospital room writing *None* next to Name of Nearest Relative.

Besides the forms, there was money. Mrs. Parker told me the nursing home wanted six hundred dollars in advance. After paying all the bills that had come in for the last month and buying the cat food, I had just a hundred twelve dollars and sixty-eight cents left in the wallet that held her money. Mother had given me a "simple ledger" to keep track of it all, and at first I thought a hundred twelve sixty-eight was a lot, until Mother pointed out that was all Aunt Aggie would have had to spend that month on food for herself, vet bills, medicines, clothes, or repairs to the house in case anything broke. I remembered then the crooked shutters, the peeled paint, the dripping kitchen faucet, and how I, like the people who said, "Isn't that a shame?" had wondered why she didn't get them fixed. I knew why now, and getting six hundred dollars before Monday seemed impossible. Mrs. Parker went along with me to talk to Aunt Aggie about it. "Perhaps you could sell some of your stocks, Agnes," she suggested. "Do you know a stockbroker?"

But Aunt Aggie shook her head. "I got that money," she said.

"Well, that's nice," answered Mrs. Parker, not quite as if she believed it. "What does Jo have to do to get it for you?"

Aunt Aggie gave me a sly, sideways look. "You mean you don't know? I thought you was writin' that story about me."

"I am, I still am. But what's that got to do with it?"

"And ain't you gone through my box? I told you that's whayuh I keep my paypuhs."

"I looked for photos," I admitted. "And I found the stocks in the bottom. And the jewelry. I've been meaning to talk to you about the box, actually. My parents say that stuff is too valuable to leave in an empty house."

"What you want me to do with it?"

"I guess it should be in the bank, really."

"Bank? Well, maybe. But right now I got a bettuh idea. You take that box to youa house—yes, I mean it, get someone to drive ya, it's heavy. Then you go through it—real careful. I think you'll be able to take 'em that six hundred, all right. And mind you get a receipt," she added after a minute. "Some people'll rob yuh as soon as look at yuh."

CHAPTER 16

THE three of us sat on the floor by the wood stove in the living room that evening, and got the cash out of Aunt Aggie's box. Inside dusty envelopes, between the pages of calendars for forgotten years, bundled up with receipts and deeds and expired insurance policies, was the money. We made a little pile of it on the cool gray slate of the hearth, and then put a brick on the pile after Watermelon came and tried to lie down on it. There were tens and fives and ones and twenties, fifties, and a few hundreds. Several were tucked inside greeting cards as if they had been birthday or Christmas gifts. *A happy holiday to Agnes from Beatrice,* said one with a twenty and a five in it. "I bet that's from Mrs. Langley," I commented. "Before Aunt Aggie stopped speaking to her."

Some had little notes clipped to them. *From Mrs. Robbins for bedstead,* said one of the hundred-dollar bills. *Kitten for Jensen,* said a grubby five. The bills were scattered all through the box, in no sort of order, and I could see that was what, more than anything else, my mother couldn't get over.

"But how could she *tell*? How could she tell how much she had?"

And Dad would answer, "Lou, honey, not everyone is a bookkeeper," and then, "I don't suppose she wanted to know, really."

There was a feeling in the house that night as if something tight had been loosened. Maybe more people were buying books. Dad joined in instead of brooding over the TV, and Mother made them café mocha and sat very close to him. I longed to ask them what had happened, but it's one of Mother's rules that kids should never have to deal with grown-ups' problems. So here I was, worrying about all sorts of things for Aunt Aggie, and not knowing what was really going on in my own family. Still, I was grateful for that evening together. There was even a little snow outside. Nothing much, just enough to hiss on the windows and make a wedding veil out of the streetlight.

It took a long time to go through the whole box, and just when we thought we were done, I discovered ten dollars tucked inside an otherwise empty leather key case. It had been like Christmas, and yet not, because there was something so private about that hidden money. A couple of times we almost caught ourselves whispering, and Mother even got up and pulled together the faded green curtains on the window that faced the street.

When everything was back in the box, Mother and I counted the money together. There was two thousand, two hundred forty-five dollars. I had never seen that much cash before, but this time I thought what it meant: a whole life's savings. I divided quickly in my head: somewhere around twenty-five dollars for every year of her life. Or, to look at it another way, less than four months in the nursing home.

But at least it was enough for what we needed now. Dad put the cash in the locked drawer of his desk and Mother made out an official receipt, which we all signed. "Received in cash from Agnes Cully Pease of 15 Oak Street, Vicinity, Massachusetts, two thousand, two hundred forty-five dollars and no/100 ($2,245.00)" and the date. "Received?" I asked. "But we're not going to keep it."

"Of course not. You're going to give her this receipt tomorrow to show that we have the money and it's hers any time she wants it. Which, by the way, had better be soon. She's *got* to have a bank account."

On Monday, right on schedule, Aunt Aggie went to the Sunnydale Convalescent Home, on Jane Street, just down the hill in back of the town hall. I had been there the previous Saturday with the six hundred dollars, which I delivered to the administrator in her ground-floor office. I was surprised when I met her, because she didn't remind me at all of Mrs. Parker or Ms. Melander or my mother, which means, I guess, that she didn't seem the type to administer things. She was pale and thin and about forty, but she wore dull, floppy clothes she might have borrowed from her patients and she spoke in a faint, uncertain voice, as if she expected to be contradicted at any moment. I guessed she never had to deal with kids and so had decided to treat me like somebody's middle-aged next of kin, or maybe that was the only way she knew to treat anybody.

She showed me around the "facilities," although I certainly hadn't asked for a tour, and I went away remembering the tables all set with large spoons, the TVs blaring game shows, and the old man who lay in bed shouting at the walls, rather than the balanced diets, sunny rooms, and friendly staff she had meant me to see.

I went home and looked up *foreboding* in the dictionary to make sure I was right about the way I was feeling. Then for good measure I looked up *creosote,* and found that it's sticky black stuff like tar. I reminded myself to mention it to Billy when I saw him that night. I had discovered he came every Wednesday and Saturday evening, as well as mornings for the stove. Then I went upstairs intending to write a poem about a girl who has second sight but only foresees disasters so nobody wants her around. Halfway through the poem, I remembered something about Cassandra. The encyclopedia confirmed it: she was the girl in the Greek story who foretold the fall of Troy. There is nothing more depressing than discovering your idea is thousands of years old.

The minute I walked into Sunnydale on Monday afternoon, I knew I could set up as a Cassandra anytime I wanted to. I could actually hear Aunt Aggie's voice from halfway down the corridor, and it was the voice that had sent fourteen cats scurrying when it wanted to.

"I didn't come heyuh to stay in bed, I tell you; I come heyuh to walk. That doctuh told me exuhcise, an' exuhcise is what I'm gonta do, but I need help. Now, you gonna help me uh not?" She sounded much angrier than she had that day in the hospital. She had been partly enjoying that; she wasn't enjoying this one bit. I walked in through fluttering nurses and found Aunt Aggie sitting bolt upright in bed, glaring like the hawk that has raided the pigeon coop.

I was not wearing my usual jeans that afternoon because the air had gone unexpectedly warm, the way it does sometimes in late February, and I had honored it by putting on purple tights and my favorite heather plaid skirt. Probably it made me look older, or maybe the administrator had given everybody the idea that I was in fact Aunt Aggie's next of kin. Anyway, I found three nurses looking at me hopefully, like kids waiting for Mommy to decide who gets the next turn on the swing, and I looked back at them and asked, "Is there a problem?"

The stout nurse said, "It's suppertime now."

The rosy nurse said, "She wants to walk."

The gray-haired nurse said, "The physiotherapist doesn't come until tomorrow."

"What time tomorrow?" I asked.

"Nine-thirty."

"Then I guess she can start walking tomorrow morning as soon as the therapist is through, right?" They nodded like a row of dolls. "Good." I said. "Aunt Aggie, you can't walk at suppertime, you'll bump into people with trays."

The nurses all looked at me as if I'd waved a wand, and in fact I was surprised I didn't get more argument from Aunt Aggie, but she only settled back against the cranked-up mattress after the nurses had left and remarked, "Well, this's a zoo, ain't it?"

"What do you mean?"

"You *know* what I mean. Look around. And listen." It was true that from down the hall I could hear a pleading voice saying, "Please come back, please come back, please come back," with a little whimper at the end of each phrase, and that the woman in the next bed was asleep and gurgling with a noise like a clogged drain. Rattling carts with supper trays were wheeled down the hall, the radiator by the bed was clanking, and over all was the sound of gunshots and laughter from a dozen television sets. I sat down on her bed and suddenly knew I wouldn't try to cheer her up with lies.

"Okay," I said, "so it's a zoo. A zoo you have to work hard to get out of. Just remember, your babies miss you and you can't take care of them till your leg is stronger. So if the doctor said for you to walk, you do it as much as you can. *I* want to see you out in your garden when it warms up."

And then we talked about the thaw, and the new snow that was sure to follow, and the chances for an early spring. "I'll be home in time fuh the crocuses," she decided, "and the jonquils. These ones Lily sent me"—she nodded at a bright bunch of daffodils on her windowsill— "are real nice, but they nevuh smell like the fresh ones."

That week, I finally persuaded her to open a bank account. The head teller at the bank sat down with me and explained all the different kinds of accounts and then helped me fill out the forms for Aunt Aggie to "sign." I had never admitted to anyone that I was doing Aunt Aggie's signature, but I thought the teller guessed because once I had slipped up and signed something at the bank counter instead of taking it to Aunt Aggie first. I thought that Mrs. Pardeau and I were in some ways alike, since I had once seen her write Mr. Follett the bank manager's initials on bank forms when he was "in conference" with his wife on the phone. Mother said he secretly read cowboy westerns. I didn't know what the head teller read, but I would have guessed it would be *The Wall Street Journal.* She certainly seemed to know more about running the bank than Mr. Follett did.

Now I was *really* busy with Aunt Aggie's affairs, because there was no more paying bills in cash; the checks had to be signed by me. I realized I had landed myself a job for life. No one else knew our secret. I began to wish that someone else would take over feeding the animals, or at least buying the food. It seemed to me that almost every afternoon Boots and I were hauling cat food in his little red wagon over icy, slushy streets.

The next time I met Billy at the house on Oak Street, I tried to raise the subject with him. We had come to be friends in a way, although I had to talk quietly and slowly or he would get frightened. Today I had some money to give him. It seemed Aunt Aggie paid him fifty cents a day for taking care of the stove and the trash. I handed him his three-fifty in an envelope when he was through with the trash. "Say, Billy, would you like to go to the store for me someday? If I gave you some money, would you buy some food for Dolly and her friends?"

"The store?"

I always wondered as I watched Billy thinking—at what age did I learn to keep from showing every one of my thoughts? Some age, perhaps, that Billy would never reach. I saw puzzlement, recollection, anticipation, and finally regret follow each other across his round face. "Billy can't go to the store." Sadness, said the face. Brave acceptance. "Billy took some candy once." Remorse. Joy returning. "Momma buys it now." Solemn awe. "Even when I'm bad." Trust. Confidence. "Mamma loves Billy." He turned away smiling and went to get the coal. It was the most I'd heard him say at one time. Is that one way to be happy, I wondered—knowing exactly what you can and can't do?

I went back to opening cans while Billy finished with the stove and went into the animal room to find Dolly. He came out almost immediately. "That pussy is dead," he said.

I almost cut myself on the can top I was bending back.

"What did you say?"

He didn't look frightened, only a little worried. "Pussy is dead," he explained. "On the bed."

It looked as if Mummy were only asleep in her favorite place, but when I bent over the stained pillow I could see she wasn't breathing and one of her eyes was half open. Her thin-striped fur felt like a blanket loosely laid over a few sharp bones.

I collapsed on the bed and burst into tears. I put the heels of my hands over my eyes, bent my head down, and cried with my whole body, while on the end of the bed, not three feet away, sat Midnight, his spine elegantly curled, one back leg stuck straight out so he could clean his toes.

But even the sound of my own sobbing could not drown out the sound of Billy saying, louder and louder, "Johanna, don't cry. Johanna, don't cry." And then in tones of alarm, *"Billy didn't do it. Billy didn't do it!"* I looked up and saw him backing out of the room as if to escape punishment.

I got to my feet feeling old—as old as Mummy, as old as Aunt Aggie. "No, no," I said, "of course you didn't do it. Of course not. She was an old cat, that's all. She was twenty-one and she was so old that she died. Do you understand?" He nodded a little. Now that he was sure no one was mad at him, he wanted to make me feel better.

"Don't cry, Johanna. Billy knows what to do. Aunt Aggie showed him."

"You mean you know what to do with the—the dead kitty?"

He nodded again, eagerly because he could see my relief. Then, as I finished my feeding, trying not to look at the pathetic little heap of fur on the bed, he asked in a small voice, "Johanna?"

"Hmm?"

"Are people same as cats?"

He could have meant anything. Certainly people were *less human* than cats to Aunt Aggie. I said slowly, "Cats and people are both alive, I guess. And they both like warm houses and good food and somebody to love them. But cats are smaller than people and they can't talk or—" I had been going to say *read.* "Or open doors and run stoves, like us. Was that what you meant?"

"But, Johanna, do they die the same?"

Suddenly I saw. "Oh, no, Billy. People live *much longer* than cats."

Relief. Reassurance. "Oh, good. That's good. 'Cause Billy's twenty-one now. He had a birthday."

When I was home on my windowseat, I cried again. It wasn't entirely for Mummy.

CHAPTER 17

"AUNT Aggie, Mummy is dead. Billy and I found her on your bed yesterday evening." I hadn't wanted to tell her over the phone.

Her mouth opened and her eyes filled with tears, but she said the last thing I expected. "On my bed?"

"Yes. She was all curled up on your pillow."

"On my pillow." She almost smiled. "Oh, the deyuh little thing. They'll mostly hide, you know, when they feel they'uh goin'. But she wanted to be with me. Oh, my. I'm goin' ta miss huh terrible." And then she cried.

All that week, I went to see Aunt Aggie every evening because there was so much to do and because I was getting worried about her. Not that I could be sure what was bothering me. In fact, I told myself one or twice that the nursing home might be getting to me as much as it was to her. Some of her complaints were just complaints, the sort I wrote home to my parents the time I went to a summer camp I didn't like. The food was no good, the TVs were too loud, the nurses didn't come fast enough.

Then there was "that one." That's what Aunt Aggie called the old woman who shared her room. She had a thin, sweet smile and neatly styled gray hair, but her conversation had no relation to what was going on around her. The first time she said to me politely, "Would you care for a cup of coffee?" I felt a surge of guilty pleasure because my mother doesn't think I should have coffee very often and I love it, but Aunt Aggie hissed at me, "She ain't talkin' to you."

I looked at the pale brown eyes focusing somewhere past my left shoulder and saw that Aunt Aggie was right. "That one," she said significantly, "is gaga. I don't know what they're aftuh, puttin' me with huh." Aunt Aggie's own eyes were a mixture of green and brown and blue, like the pebbles you find at the beach. They could be hard as pebbles, but pebbles, I reminded myself, took a long time to wear down.

Sometimes, those evenings, she was restless and grumpy, telling me no one came to see her anymore and even hinting it was my fault she was there instead of at home. She went back to fretting about Frosty, too, and once she startled me by complaining about God. "It's wicked. Don't you think it's wicked of God to let this happen to me?" I had no answer to that one.

Other times, she seemed sleepy and wouldn't answer me when I asked what she wanted done with a piece of mail. She said they were giving her too many pills, and I remembered how she used to boast she never took anything except senna (whatever that was) for her bowels and grape juice for her "ahthuritis."

One evening after she'd been at Sunnydale a few weeks, she took hold of my forearm and pulled me down by the bed the minute I came in. "Joan. I found out somethin'."

"What's that, Aunt Aggie?"

She glanced toward the door, as if to make sure "that one" was asleep and no nurses were within earshot. *"No one heyuh's goin' home."*

"What do you mean?"

"I mean none of 'em's goin' home. They're all heyuh *puhmanent."*

At that moment we were interrupted by Mrs. Parker, who had stopped by with some homemade gingerbread on her way from work. "Agnes, you're not very chipper tonight," she said after they had chatted a minute.

"No, I ain't feelin' good, an' that's a fact. It's the noise in this place, you know. A body can't get any rest."

"Oh, they all say that in the beginning. You'll get

so you don't notice it." Mrs. Parker could be very hearty when she wanted to. "And how's the hip? You walking good?"

But that, as I could have told her, was another of Aunt Aggie's complaints. She would have walked a lot more, she said, if the nurses hadn't been too busy to help her. "Ten minutes in the mohnin' ain't enough, but they got this *schedule* they go by."

Mrs. Parker and I left together, and I said to her as we went down the walk, past the one stone bench and the two pots spiky with dead black chrysanthemum stems, "Is she really all right in there?"

"Well, Jo, she's fed and she's clothed, and she's clean. She wouldn't be any of those things if she were home right now. At the same time, she isn't getting on as fast as I'd hoped, I'll admit. You know, Doc Warnke has said all along there was a good chance she'd never walk by herself again, and maybe he's right. Look, get in the car and I'll buy us a cup of coffee, it's freezing out here." We went into the warm, vanilla-smelling drugstore on Main Street, and sat down at the U-shaped fountain. *Coffee.* I felt very grown up and only a little guilty about what my mother would say.

"I've been thinking," said Mrs. Parker, nodding her red head to show how hard she'd been working at it. "In social work there's something called *advocacy,* Jo. It means taking somebody's part, presenting their point of view even when it isn't your own. I think you're going to have to be Aggie's advocate.

She can't do it herself because she gets mad and they don't listen. I can't do it because I work for another institution and it would be butting in. But you can do it."

"But what do I do? And what do I say?"

"If I were you, I'd start with the head nurse. Pat Masetti, her name is. She runs a good place, but she's overworked, like every other nurse I ever knew. Tell her Aggie's problem about the walking. God knows, they ought to be glad to have somebody with gumption over there. They get past a certain stage, you know, and they just sit. And while you're at it, ask her what medication they have Aggie on. Sometimes, just between you and me, they hand out a few too many tranquilizers; it keeps the place quieter. You write down the names and show them to me because you won't know what they are."

She looked at her watch, a tiny gold one that seemed lost on her strong, freckled wrist. "Uh-oh, I have to get back to the zoo, it's feeding time. Those boys'll eat the furniture if I don't make with the meatballs, and oh, my aching feet. Can I give you a ride home?"

But I was going to Oak Street, which was in the opposite direction, so she paid for our coffee, pulled up the hood of her quilted purple coat, and bounced out to her car, aching feet or not.

I walked to Aunt Aggie's house thinking about advocacy. *Taking someone's part.* Aunt Aggie had been an advocate for animals all her life. If she needed someone to be an advocate for her now, I would do it.

I took care of the animals quickly, then went home and up to my room. Mother found me a few minutes later in front of the bathroom mirror. That was so unusual that she put her head in and asked, "What's going on, hon?"

"Oh, nothing. I was just wondering, does doing this with my hair make me look older?" I had pulled my hair up on top of my head in a knot.

"How old did you have in mind?"

"How old do you have to be not to be a minor?"

"Eighteen. Well . . . it does make you look older, but I can't say it's very flattering."

"I just need to talk to someone for Aunt Aggie. I wasn't going to parade down the runway in Atlantic City."

"Johanna Justine, the things you *say*!"

"Last fall," I reminded her, "you were worried that I was too quiet." I looked at her, short and neat in her business clothes, curly black hair just a little gray, hazel eyes just a little worried behind her glasses. I was so much taller now, I could see the straight line of her part running all the way back. I would be even taller when I put on my one pair of high heels to go see Mrs. Masetti.

" 'Too quiet,' " said my mother, as if reminding herself. "Yes, you're right. And too uninvolved, too, that's what I said. Was it only last fall? Well, don't change too much, darling, will you? And don't muss my hair either," she added as I hugged her, "we're going over to the Brecks' for dinner."

The cold weather that had made Mrs. Parker buy me the coffee was almost the last of the season. March was going out, not exactly like a lamb but more like a fish, snow melting everywhere and storm drains clogged with little icebergs so that people's backyards and cellars turned into ponds and Dad said he was thinking of buying a canoe to get across the parking lot at the bookstore.

My meeting with Mrs. Masetti had come off all right, with her agreeing that Aunt Aggie should have more time to walk. "It's nice to see a little git up 'n go," she said, echoing Mrs. Parker almost exactly. "I'll assign two of the girls to get her up again in the afternoons." About the pills, she had been less helpful, although she wrote down the names and doses for me. "We have doctor's orders for everything," she said. "He only prescribes what's best for the patient. There's nothing at all I can do."

The earliest spring is almost my favorite time of year because it's like a treasure hunt. Not even finding the money in Aunt Aggie's "box" was as exciting as watching for the first little green points in the grass, the first gold or red in the tree buds. The daylight lasted longer now, and Boots and I went on all sorts of muddy expeditions—to the bridge over the Squanatisset to see the ice going out, to the swamp to check for pussy willows, to the Kerners' barn to pet the new calf. I was puzzled at Boots's lack of interest in Aunt Aggie. He never mentioned her name, even when we passed her house. One afternoon we found our first snowdrop, in a sunny spot in front of the library, and I told him, "Aunt Aggie said she'd be coming home for the crocuses. She'd better hurry up, hunh?"

Boots was watching a shiny brown beetle struggle out from under a piece of bark in the library flower bed. He said indifferently, "Aunt Aggie's never coming home."

"Hey, what makes you say that?"

"People don't. They don't come home from those places." Boots put his hand in front of the beetle and watched it climb up the finger, over the chubby knuckle, and onto the back of his hand.

"Why, Bootsie, who told you that?"

"My mommy. They take you away in a amyulance and put tubes in you and you die. Johanna, where is it that beetles do their eyes?"

I would have liked to take this easy way out, but I couldn't. "Bootsie, listen to me. I think you didn't understand your mommy. Lots of people go in the hospital and come out again all well. I don't know for sure about Aunt Aggie"—better get it said so there's no broken promise later— "but all of us are hoping *real hard* that she'll be able to come home soon and see you and give you fruit drops again."

"My grandaddy didn't," he said. He blew the

beetle off his hand. It landed on its back and began to struggle wildly. "See ya later, crocodile," he added. It was a new expression of his, but he often got it wrong. *Oh, boy,* I thought. First Billy, Then Boots. But to Boots, at three and a half, I didn't know what to say.

Spring came for certain, though, and Aunt Aggie was still at Sunnyvale. One Saturday, Mother and I raked leaves out of the front garden on Oak Street and Mother went around exclaiming at what she saw coming up. "That gray-green stuff is Dutchman's-breeches, and the flat green is partridgeberry. The light green spikes are daylily, of course, and my goodness, I think that's hepatica. I didn't know that even grew wild around here. She must have found a lot of these things in the woods. Those with the purple edges are going to be spiderwort, tradescantia is the other name, and—would you believe it—there's an Easter lily?"

"What's amazing about that?"

"Nothing, except you can't grow them outdoors this far north, all the books say so. But there it is."

I was almost through, now, with my paper about Aunt Aggie for the local-history class. At about the same time, I finished the mad-scientist story I had dreamed up in the hospital corridor back in February. I brought it to school one day to show Jenny. She gave me back a poem—not about spring or sunsets, the way she'd recommended to me, but about cutting a Christmas tree with her father. We were sitting around after the local-history group, just sort of soaking up the sun that poured in through the high windows. It had been weeks since I'd given up scurrying straight home from school every day. The things Ms. Melander made happen were just too interesting.

Jason and a couple of other kids from the group were looking at a map he'd drawn on the board showing his latest idea about the missing tombstones, when Jenny said, "Why doesn't this stupid school have a literary magazine, anyway?"

"I don't know," I said, half asleep, "but it sure ought to. The school my friend goes to in Belmont does."

One of the kids at the blackboard was the skinny faculty brat named Dan. "You want to know why no magazine?" he asked. "Why do you think? Because Jock Strap doesn't want one and he's the head of the English department."

"So what's he got against literachaw?" asked Jason, who didn't have Stropner for English. "I have a whole drawerful of science fiction I'd sure like to get out."

Dan shrugged.

"I don't think," said Lucinda Cray unexpectedly, "that Mr. Stropner considers the writing of fiction and poetry to be a productive pursuit." Was Lucinda trying to be funny or was that just the way she talked?

Jenny sat up from the desk she'd been lying on and crossed her legs under her. "Is there anything to prevent somebody from just *starting* a magazine if they wanted to?"

"You'd need an advisor."

"We could ask Melander. I bet she'd say yes."

"You got one problem," said Dan, collecting his books and getting ready to go.

"Yeah? What's that?"

"Ever read that pamphlet they give you every fall? 'Regulations Relating to Extracurricular Activities'? It says in there you can do anything you want, with any advisor you want, *but* it has to be approved in writing by the head of the relevant department."

"So?" said Lucinda in her usual snippy way.

"So this," said Dan patiently. " 'Relevant department' means English. You want to start a Ping-Pong club, you gotta go through athletics. You want a magazine, you go through English. Can you really imagine old Jock Strap letting you start a magazine with somebody else?"

"Buy why should he care?" said Lucinda, sounding genuinely bewildered.

I sat up as the door slammed behind Dan and a couple of others who hadn't joined the discussion. Now there were only five of us—Jenny, Jason, Lucinda, me, and a quiet black girl named Elizabeth Viney, who was researching Vicinity's role in the Underground Railroad.

"He would care," I said, answering Lucinda's

question, "because he objects to things he can't control, one. And he wouldn't like the idea that anybody wasn't totally satisfied with his own wonderful, prizewinning way of teaching 'workable prose,' two."

"I draw," said Elizabeth in a soft voice. Her eyes were big and dreamy. "I draw cartoons. And other stuff. Could I draw for your magazine?"

"Haven't you been listening, Lize?" said Jenny. "There probably isn't going to be any magazine."

"Nuts to that," said Jason. "I'm not ready to give up yet. If we want a magazine, I say there's going to be one."

I picked up Boots that afternoon and we went to the town field with his red wagon. There's a playground there, and also a long grassy slope that you can sled or ride a wagon down. The temperature must have been almost sixty. It was the kind of day when I imagined a bear coming out of its winter den and wanting to throw off its ratty old fur coat.

For a while Boots and I were almost alone on the playground. There was only one mother there, with a small baby and a little girl about Boots's age. The two of them got down to some serious sand digging, and I climbed to the top of the slide and lay on my back with my hands just holding on over my head at the top. My body felt long and loose and strangely good. Above me was nothing but sky and the bee-drone of a tiny jet plane.

Like the hibernating bear, I had spent a cold, dark winter alone. Like a bee, I had come staggering into the sun to find that I was not alone after all.

After a while the little girl and her mother and the baby went away, and Boots wanted to ride his wagon. He headed for the slope, then veered off toward a clump of trees by the edge of the field. "Where're you going?" I called, but he decided not to hear. Spring has got to him, too, I thought. I sideslipped down the slope after him. In a few seconds I saw what had attracted his attention. Four or five boys had come out of the trees. They were rolling a black plastic garbage can along on its bottom. Every few steps, they'd stop and look into the can. Boots reached them first, and I heard him say, "Can I see?" One of the boys obligingly hoisted him up. "Wowee!" said Boots, "is it a biting one?"

I had just got close enough to see what they were looking at. Inside the can was a large snapping turtle. It must have come from the pond that lay between the field and the railroad tracks. I recognized one of the boys as Mack Parker. "How did you catch it?" I asked him.

"Mikey found it," he said, nodding at a stringy, dark kid. "It was just crawlin' through the woods."

"So we went to my house," explained Mikey, gesturing up toward Main Street, "an' got the tongs an' the can." He held up a pair of black iron fire tongs.

"Man, did he hiss!" said a third boy. "He's a mean old thing."

The turtle was so big, it almost covered the bottom of the trash can, but it scrabbled constantly at the edges with its flat brown feet. They had claws larger than a cat's, and the blunt jaws at the end of its ancient, snakelike head looked like a pair of wire cutters. Its mouth was open and ready to bite, plenty big enough for a human finger, and its eyes were mad and yellow. I remembered hearing that snapping turtles ate whole fish and snakes, and even baby ducks.

The turtle tore at the hard plastic and hissed with a sound like air coming out of a bicycle tire. Then it lay quiet a minute, its throat pulsing in and out as it panted. But the minute the boys started off again with the can toward Mikey's house, it threw itself into a fresh fury of clawing and snapping.

Boots watched them go, wishing he were big enough for such adventures. "See ya later, crocodile," he said, waving.

CHAPTER 18

THAT evening when I got home, Dad said I'd had a phone message to see Mr. Follett at the bank.

"Oh, no!" I groaned. "I must have made a mistake with Aunt Aggie's checkbook or something. Maybe she's overdrawn."

That was still what I was thinking about when I arrived at the bank the next afternoon. The bank building used to be a house, and the manager's office is in what must have been the best room in it. There's a fireplace, polished wood paneling, and a general atmosphere that reminds you of a historical museum with red velvet ropes on all the chairs. Mr. Follett has beautiful white hair and looks so much like a bank manager, I might have figured he had to be a plumber or a terrorist.

He started by saying how kind and well-meaning I was to do things for Mrs. Pease, whom he called "that poor old soul," but I could tell he was aiming at something else, and eventually he got to it.

"It has come to my attention that you, a minor, have been walking out of here with substantial sums of money without anything except verbal authorization—authorization from someone who may not always be, let us say, entirely clear in her mind." He stopped and held up a pink, manicured hand as if I had objected, but I just went on sitting. "Now, of course you know and I know that every cent of that money has gone where it should have, but as you must appreciate, banking deals in certainties and not in faith." He shook his head in horror.

"But Mrs. Pease has an account now," I said. "No one will be cashing her checks anymore." Then my stomach winced as I saw the trap I'd fallen into.

"Ah, yes. About that account. I was examining the checks from Mrs. Pease's file just the other day. It is certainly remarkable how her signature has changed recently. Not deteriorated: changed." Again he waited, but since I didn't say anything he went on again. "Now, what can we do about all this?" He tried out a fatherly smile on me. "It seems to me that if Mrs. Pease can't sign her own checks for whatever reason, mental or physical, then all she needs to do is execute a power of attorney in favor of some responsible adult, perhaps her lawyer. Certainly a minor cannot exercise such authority." He reached out and patted my knee before I could stop him. Suddenly, he was all smiles. "Naturally, I realize all this can't be arranged overnight. I'm prepared to let the present arrangement go until, say, the end of the month."

He was letting me go. I muttered a few words, and scuttled out the door trying to figure out if I was more mad than scared or more scared than mad. Things had been working so well and I had felt so good about getting Aunt Aggie to open that bank account. Now I wished I hadn't done it. One thing was sure: If I couldn't sign her checks anymore, she was trapped.

A couple of blocks down Main Street, I passed a driveway with a familiar-looking black garbage can. The turtle was inside it—dead. Its brown back had dried grayish and dull, its fierce old head flopped against the side of its prison, and it had torn two toes off one front foot in its panicky efforts to escape the trap. But its eyes, though filmed over now, were open and yellow. Unlike the cat on Aunt Aggie's bed, it had died fighting.

I was angry. The boys had been cruel or thoughtless, it didn't matter which. But after all, what had I done to stop them? If I went and yelled at them now, they wouldn't even understand why. It was only a mean old turtle, not a cute furry pussycat.

It was the same with Aunt Aggie, wasn't it? Who minded what happened to a grouchy, lonely old woman? *See ya later, crocodile,* I thought as I walked on to Boots's house. *See ya later, crocodile.*

When I got to the nursing home that evening, I found Aunt Aggie had the flu. Just when the bad weather had gone and the flowers were starting. The nurse at the front desk told me she was running a temperature and I shouldn't stay long, so I kept my bad news and just chatted a minute.

"It's no wonduh I caught this," she said huskily. "They all got it. I'm the fifth case this week." Suddenly she said fiercely, "I'd never of got this if I was home with my babies. Fifteen years, I wasn't sick a day." Her eyes were red, and her hand felt hot when I patted it.

The next day I got another message in school. Mrs. Parker called to say Aunt Aggie had just been readmitted to the hospital. "It's nothing to worry too much about, Jo. She's got a good strong heart and she's holding up fine. But they heard some congestion in her lungs, and at her age you don't fool around with that. They've got her on oxygen but you can go see her if you want to."

In fact, I didn't get to see Aunt Aggie for a couple of days because some other things happened. First, I went in her dining room that day to get a roll of paper towels (there was a case of them on top of the sideboard) and found a small puddle in the middle of the dining table. While I stood staring at it, a drop fell into it, and I looked up at the ceiling to see a damp patch on the plaster and a little crack with another drop forming in it. I tore off a wad of the paper towel I'd come for, left it to soak up the puddle, and went upstairs. It had been raining hard all day, and I supposed there must be a leak in the roof. I checked the bathroom, with its dusty rolls of wallpaper and cartons of junk, but everything was dry. The leak must be in the room next to the bathroom, which I had never been into. At first I thought the door was stuck, but then I saw the old-fashioned keyhole and wondered if it was locked. I remembered the bunch of keys that always hung in the front hall over the light switch—not outside door keys, but the key that wound the parlor clock and a set of car keys that had once belonged to Aunt Aggie's ancient Hudson. As I had thought, there were some door keys on it too. I took them back upstairs, and the second one I tried fitted.

The room I walked into was so small, it must have been meant as a dressing room, since it could never have held a bed. There was a bare bulb in a wall bracket by the door. I found the switch and turned it on, getting dust on my fingers. Like all the rest of the upstairs, the room was very warm with heat rising from the stove in the kitchen. I stood looking into it for a minute, wondering why I was suddenly uneasy. The house felt too quiet, the air too still. I listened hard but heard nothing except the rain on the roof and the thump of a cat jumping off something in the animal room. I hugged myself with my arms and told myself I'd been hearing too much about haunted houses from Jason and Phil. After all, there was nothing whatsoever in the room except a tall painted chest of drawers whose handles were carved like pieces of fruit. I walked around behind it and saw the leak—dripping from a crack in the ceiling by the window, oozing across the worn, speckled linoleum, and disappearing under the chest. I stepped around to one side and tried to lift it, but the wood was too smooth. I pulled open a drawer so I could lift from the inside.

I never put my hand in that drawer.

Inside, curled as neatly as when I last saw it, lay the body of Aunt Aggie's cat Mummy.

There was nothing especially awful about it, just a faint sick smell that must have reached my brain before my nose bothered to tell me about it. The little body was lying there on a clean sheet of newspaper, but I felt my face grow hot and then prickle with sweat while a hard feeling rose in the back of my throat and my breath came out in a gasp. Without noticing that I had moved, I found myself with my back against the wall, looking at Aunt Aggie's last secret.

Or was it the last? Slowly, I went forward and pulled open the other drawers. Mummy was not alone. There were two other cats in the chest—a gaunt black one that I vaguely remembered dying of pneumonia when I first knew Aunt Aggie, and a long-haired gray one I had never seen before. They lay on their sides, as dry and empty as cast-off gloves, waiting, I supposed, for Billy to come with his boxes and creosote. ("Don't cry, Johanna. Billy knows what to do.") I didn't want to think about the details, but of course that didn't keep me from doing so.

I shut the drawers, wiped up what water I could reach, and put a white china pitcher from the bathroom under the leak. Then I closed the door behind me and went down to the kitchen. The way to the cellar was beside the stove, and there was a light pull at the top of the stairs. I had to shut the door behind me to keep the animals from following me. But though the air from the cellar gusted up cold and moldy, I made myself go halfway down. The cellar was small, and it was easy to spot what I was looking for.

On a bench opposite the furnace stood fourteen pale wooden boxes, about two feet long and six inches high. Six were empty; eight had their tops nailed shut with shiny, brass-headed nails, and the same nails had been used to make crosses on the lids. In the cracks of the wood you could just see a few beads of creosote. On the side of each box was a name in large, penciled letters. BONNIE, BUTCH, SNOWY, FLUFFY . . . I didn't stay to read them all.

As I walked home with the rain battering on Dad's old black umbrella, I thought that I had seen a lot of odd things recently and that perhaps for a while I wouldn't write any more horror stories.

The next day Mr. Stropner turned down our request to start a literary magazine with Ms. Melander as advisor. "He said," reported Jenny furiously, "that he didn't see a useful purpose for it and that we were just, just—"

"Dissipating," prodded Lucinda. "He said we'd be dissipating our energies."

"Hey, great! I've always wanted to be dissipated!" crowed Jason.

"That's right," Jenny went on. "And that a magazine would never get past the kickoff anyway—his words—that he'd seen a lot of projects like this and they never scored."

"What a bunch of bull," said Jason, sounding discouraged. "All he really cares about is his dumb comp test scores."

"It doesn't even make sense," said Elizabeth, who had a talent for logic. "If we dissipated our energies, we'd have to be producing something. If we lost interest and didn't produce anything—no wasted energy." Ms. Melander had been sitting quietly at her desk while Jenny and Lucinda gave their report. Now she hooked one elbow over the back of her chair, pointed the finger of the other hand at us, and delivered a summary. "In a situation like this, you have only two choices: You can give up or you can keep on. If you keep on, you have two other choices: You can make the opposition change its mind or you can change the ground rules of the situation. Again, mind-changing involves either persuasion or intimidation. That leaves you four clean-cut alternatives to consider. Do that, and we'll discuss this further next time." She looked at her watch and got up quickly. "I'm sorry, but I really have to go now."

"Gee whiz," said Lucinda as the door shut behind Melander, "what's the matter with her? I thought she was on our side."

Jenny scowled. "Honestly, Lu! I suppose it never occurred to you she might be worrying about her mother."

"Her mother?" I said. "I know her mother. What's wrong with her?"

"Oh, she had a little attack or something," said Lucinda. "I heard the kids saying it. But I don't see—"

Jenny pulled me toward the door without listening to the rest. "She had a heart attack," she explained. "My dad was on the ambulance. Not too bad, he said, but they can't always tell."

Oh, no, I thought. That nice lady. No wonder Melander left.

CHAPTER 19

I had to give the nursing home another check that afternoon, so Boots was with me when I went over.

The administrator's office was not a bit like Mr. Follett's. Her desk was scratched gray metal that matched her suit, her curtains were patterned with constipated-looking American eagles in blue and mustard, and the walnut paneling had been cut from plastic trees. There was a tall, handsome man in the office's one comfortable chair when I came to the door. The administrator introduced him as Dr. Warnke, and I saw he was one of the doctors who'd been in Aunt Aggie's room the day everyone was trying to persuade her to come to Sunnydale.

When I had finished handing over the check, with its guiltily forged signature, Dr. Warnke said, "You know, Lila, it's a lucky chance that Johanna happened to come by when she did. I've heard a lot about her and I've been wanting to have a chat with her for quite a while. Would it be all right, do you think, if we used the other office? That is, of course, if you could spare me a few minutes, Johanna."

I said something about Boots, who had been hanging around the doorway hoping I would take him to the playground. Dr. Warnke went down on one knee and stuck his finger in Boots's stomach so that he giggled. "Look here, young man, I need to talk to your baby-sitter for a few minutes, okay? I promise I won't keep her too long. And maybe, just maybe, I've got something here in my bag that you'd like." He made a great pretense of fumbling around in the medical bag he had with him and at last put two fists behind his back. From where I was standing, I could see that each held a sourball. "Which hand will you have?" Boots chose, and the doctor offered me the other one. "I keep them in my bag because I'm trying to stop smoking," he explained ruefully. "Appalling for a doctor to be such a bad example." He had dark curly hair, tanned skin, and wonderful blue eyes like a Siamese cat's.

I followed him into the little room next door and took one of the two metal chairs with turquoise plastic seats. Boots was soon happily involved with some drawing materials and the doctor's stethoscope.

Dr. Warnke was still smiling when he turned to

me. "Of course, it's about Mrs. Pease I've been wanting to talk to you. I've asked her more than once to tell you to drop by my office sometime, but no doubt she forgot. Shall I call you Johanna, or do your friends call you Jo?"

"Johanna's fine," I said. It sounded more important, or maybe more grown up, than plain Jo.

"Wonderful. I'm so glad the solid, old-fashioned names are coming back. For a while it was all Sheris and Stacys and Loris. My own little daughter is named Charlotte. Ah, well. Getting back to your friend, I wanted to reassure you first about this flu. It's nothing much, no complications. I'm sure she'll be home in a few days."

"Home?"

"Oh, dear." He looked upset. "I meant here, of course. So many of my patients do live here. Mrs. Pease would skin me for saying that. She's quite a gal, isn't she?"

"Yes, she is. She really is."

"Ah," he said, putting his head on one side. "You're very fond of her. I can't tell you how often I would like to prescribe someone exactly like you for my patients.

"Now, help me if you will, Johanna. I'm trying to get a picture of Agnes's life before the accident. In my kind of work, we sometimes use the phrase 'support systems,' meaning the help that's available beyond the institution—the hospital or nursing home."

I was pleased at Dr. Warnke's interest. Here was a real doctor who had lots of experience with old people. Perhaps he could even help me solve the problem of the check signatures.

I told him, sitting there with the glorious spring sunshine pouring in on the tacky little room, almost the whole story: the cats, the shopping, the bills, the cash and stocks in the trunk, writing letters and answering mail, Billy and the coal stove, even the forged signatures. When I got through, he stayed silent a minute, staring at the floor. Then he said gently, "It's a lot, Johanna, it's a lot of responsibility. I had no idea one person had taken on all this alone."

He had said "one person," and not "a mere child." I appreciated it. By this time, in fact, I was feeling overwhelmed, just from reciting the whole thing, but I said, to be fair, "It's not really alone. There's a Mrs. Lisle who gets Aunt Aggie's mail and Mrs. Parker at the hospital's been a real help about all the forms and things."

"Mrs. Lisle! But she's in the hospital now herself! Jim Faulkner's patient. I saw her name on the admissions list. So now you'll be having to get the mail as well."

It was the first time I had thought of it.

"And of course you have school too," he said. "A bright girl like you doesn't let the homework slide—and you baby-sit for my friend here." He grinned at Boots, who was by now drawing red scribbles on a piece of chart paper the doctor had found for him in a drawer. *"You can't keep it up, you know,"* he said suddenly. "You're bailing a leaking boat in a heavy sea. Now don't interrupt me for a minute. You've told me a very touching story—told me, perhaps, more than you know—and I want to show you how it strikes me, all right?"

He tipped his head back and ran his clasped hands over his face and hair, collecting his thoughts. He looked tired. This must be the end of a whole day of taking care of patients, here and in the hospital. At his office, too, maybe.

"Johanna, I see here an old woman with a lot of character. For a long time she kept going in conditions that would have broken down anyone else. She has no relatives, few friends, a tiny income. Her house and her animals are everything to her. Soon, without her realizing it, conditions become nearly intolerable: poor food, hazards of fire and accident, even poor sanitation. No, you didn't have to tell me that. It was easy to guess. Then comes a crisis. A fall. She might have died right there, from shock or dehydration, unable to reach the phone. But Mrs. Pease is lucky. She has a friend who is young, intelligent, and giving. The friend moves in, fills the gaps. She does all the things you have told me about, and more besides. She provides encouragement, energy, initiative. Above all, she provides the illusion of hope. I suppose you think *illusion* is a harsh word? Johanna, I ask you to see your friend as she really is."

He looked at me, and what I read in his eyes was pity. "I saw Mrs. Pease the night she was admitted. In addition to the broken hip, she had flea bites and sores on her body that were the result of her not having washed. Not because she didn't wish to, of course, but because the arthritis had restricted her movements. She also had an infected cat scratch on the back of her left leg, a painful draining wound made worse by poor circulation. Within the next week, I observed that she had tremor in her hands so bad that she surely could not write and had difficulty feeding herself.

"Now we come to her mental state. No—I can't tell you how often I've heard what you are about to say: 'But Auntie, or Mamma, or Granddad, was like that before the illness too.' Of course they were. Age, fortunately or unfortunately, does not wait for illness. It comes like a thief in the night, if you will forgive my quoting the Bible. When I deal with Agnes as a physician, I see in her the same symptoms of guile, stubbornness, and meaningless anger that I have seen in so many others. She is strong in body, but she has come to a place in her life where she needs the care and protection that only a place like this can provide. I tell you this, of course, for only one reason. I am asking you to do a very difficult thing, but I believe, having met you, that you can do it: Give your friend the chance you would, I know, give any stray animal—to be clean, to be cared for, to be fed. Don't, by your expectations, pressure her to do the impossible.

"I know you don't believe me now, but you will grow beyond this piece of your life. After all, you have barely started high school. It won't be long before you have other interests and other needs too. That's only natural. By propping her up now, you just put off the inevitable. Sometimes—and I say this out of a life somewhat longer than yours—sometimes the most loving thing looks the hardest. You have a remarkable amount of influence on Agnes. I'm hoping that you will use it wisely."

Through the window the spring sun was still shining on the anemic philodendron plant drooping over a plastic trellis in a plastic pot, on my battered blue-and-white sneaker, on Boots's gold head, not bent over his paper now but watching me with concern. "Jo-Jo?"

"Yeah?"

"Are you sadded?"

"No, Cowboy. Just thinking."

Dr. Warnke stood and looked down at me. "My dear girl, I'm so sorry. I seem to have talked your ear off. Put it down to advancing age. I'll leave you now. It's a lovely day and you two must have many better things to do than listen to a not so young doctor philosophize. It's your fault for being such a good listener." He retrieved his stethoscope from

Boots, gave him another sourball, and was almost out the door.

"Wait. Just a minute, please." He was strong and I was weak. I couldn't let him leave me in such a turmoil. "What could I do—really? I mean, suppose it was better for her to stay here? What would happen about the cats and the house and all?"

"My dear Johanna, these are big questions, and I certainly don't have instant answers. I do know there are professionals—lawyers and such—who deal with situations like this all the time. It needn't go so far as giving someone a power of attorney. (You know what that is? Good.) There are things called conservatorships. I know a lawyer here in town who handled one for a patient of mine. All it means is someone professional doing a lot of what you've been doing now. The animals, of course, will be a problem, but I have a feeling someone like you could find homes for them. I mean good homes that Agnes would approve of. Let's you and I think about it, shall we?"

Again he headed for the door. Boots and I collected our coats and went down the stairs and out into the bright sun and the cold spring wind.

I spent the rest of that day and the next with an argument going on so loudly in my head, I was surprised no one could hear it. *Not go home? Of course she has to go home. She hates that place.*

But she'd hate dying more. Suppose next time she fell she was out by the privy in that unheated shed? She'd freeze to death out there.

Advocacy: presenting someone's point of view, even when it isn't yours.

But does she really have a point of view? "Guile, stubbornness and meaningless anger," he said. He meant senility, being gaga. Remember Frosty and little Suzie Carmody. That was weird, all right. Or the dead cat part? I never told him that. Cats in bureau drawers, cats in coffins. Cash in a trunk. Calling me Joan and Boots Bobby. The conspiratorial whisper: "I found out none of them is goin' home."

Dr. Warnke was kind. He never suggested I might be getting tired of bank statements and catfood cans. But if, somehow, we get around Jock Strap, I'd never have time for all this and a magazine. Am I only agreeing with him because I want to get out of this?

Am I only disagreeing with him because I want to go on feeling important? Round and round like a cat trying to bite the middle of its own back. By the time Mother was able to give me a ride to the hospital, I almost didn't want to go.

Aunt Aggie was in a different room now. My big plastic tag said "207." Remembering the way she had been just after the accident, and Mrs. Parker's mention of an oxygen tent, I was expecting her to look terrible, but she didn't. She was sitting up in bed eating a hamburger patty with mashed peas, and though her hand still shook, the food was getting into her mouth and not on the bed. One of the nurses had tied back her hair with a piece of bright pink wool, and she was wearing a pale pink crocheted bed jacket with satin ribbons. "Lily sent that to me," she told me when I had said hello and given her my bunch of red tulips. "I saw huh go by today with a nuhse. She looks bad. *Haht,* you know."

"It's beautiful, Aunt Aggie," I said, meaning the bed jacket, "and you look fine too."

"Bettuh than I was in *that place.* Sometimes you have to get sick to get well."

"How do you mean?"

"I mean that place is poison fuh me, just poison. Cahn't get any rest, cahn't eat that slop they cook, it's all fuh folks that cahn't chew. They were amazed heyuh. Afta the fuhst day I come right along, eatin' good and all. I was even walkin' today. *Oh,* am I gointa give them a piece of my mind when I get back to that place!"

I was relieved, at least, to hear that she knew she wasn't ready to leave the nursing home. But could she be right about the place—did she get worse there, or was it just "stubbornness and meaningless anger"? I found I couldn't be with her and really believe that. Only—suppose I was wrong? I left without telling her about our problem with the bank, and certainly without mentioning Dr. Warnke. I knew perfectly well why she hadn't told me he wanted to see me: She didn't like people talking about her behind her back. ("Suspiciousness"?)

As I went down the corridor I heard a voice call my name, and there in 223 was Mrs. Lisle. Aunt

Aggie had been right. Her smile was as sweet and friendly as ever, but the pink was gone from her cheeks and there were dark pockets under her eyes that hadn't been there before. I went in to say hello and saw she was wearing a bed jacket that was almost the twin of Aunt Aggie's except it was blue. She smiled when I commented. "Lord, I've got two afghans, four shawls, and three pairs of slippers. My sister Rose, you know, she sends me something every year. 'Lily, Rose, and Violet.' Wasn't it naughty of our father to name us like that? He had no idea of the teasing we'd get in school."

"Well, I guess it was better than Petunia, Poinsettia, and Pansy."

Mrs. Lisle laughed. "My goodness, child, you do me good. Can you stay and chat a minute? Laughter's the best medicine, they do say."

I sat down, noticing that instead of cat pictures and a cigar box on her bedside table, Mrs. Lisle had a bottle of cologne, and three gothic romances, the kind with girls and ruined castles on the jackets. She saw me looking at them. "Oh, yes," she said lightly, "I still like my gothics. No matter how many years go by, you're still eighteen inside your head, you know. Not that I'm exactly ready for them to cart me away to the nursing home yet."

"Nursing home? Are you thinking of—"

"No, no, dear, of course not. Why, if that day ever comes, I'd have Rhonda and Paul's spare room. They've been after me to live with them for a year now, ever since my last attack. But I say I'll come when I'm ready, and not before."

I had picked up one of the paperbacks and was turning it over in my hands, looking at the faraway, romantic scene with waves crashing, a storm in the distance, and the wind blowing the girl's cloak.

"What is it, Johanna?" said Mrs. Lisle. "You look troubled." I remembered then that she had been a teacher like Melander, and teachers, at least good ones, have to hear a lot of other people's problems. I thought, too, that though Mrs. Lisle would know exactly why I had picked her to ask, she would not be offended. "I think I need some advice. From someone who knows Aunt Aggie. That is, if it won't tire you out?"

"Johanna, dear, I'll have eternity to be tired in. Besides, helping with someone else's problems is the next best thing to laughing at your own."

"Okay, then. Aunt Aggie's doctor thinks maybe she shouldn't go home. I mean ever."

While I told her the rest, she put her head back against the pillows and closed her eyes, but the tiny tapping movement of two of her pink-polished nails told me she listening. When I finished, she shook her head and sighed. "Johanna, I wish I could help you, I really do. But you see, what you want is for me to decide for you, or perhaps to decide for Agnes. No one can do that. But I will say you can put that business of 'not being very clear in her mind' right out of your head. Agnes never did see the world like the rest of us, that's all. I always thought she made this town a more interesting place, though she can certainly be provoking when she gets started. Poor Bea Langley!

"But this other business, of course, I don't know. Anyone can tell that house is a booby trap in many ways. Why, just walking through all those animals could trip a person up."

"Oh, well," I said, "thank you anyway. I'll tell Dr. Warnke what you said about her not having changed."

"Warnke, dear? Did you say Warnke? Oh, my, why didn't I think?" She was frowning.

"Why? What is it about Dr. Warnke?"

"Johanna, I apologize. At my age I sometimes forget that not everyone has had the benefit of a lifetime of gossip. Now listen carefully. Nursing homes don't just grow. Somebody builds them and owns them and makes money from them. In the case of Sunnydale those somebodies are Elmer Robb—you know Robb Real Estate on Main Street?—and Dr. Regis Warnke. You can figure out the rest for yourself."

"You don't mean he might try to keep her there when she was perfectly all right?"

"Of course not, dear, that would be *wicked.* Regis is a good doctor, I'm sure. His mother was a fine person. But what you must ask yourself is whether he's *open-minded.* Most people in this world aren't, when they stand to make a profit."

"But Mrs. Pease has hardly anything."

Mrs. Lisle took my hand between her own and patted it. "Now you've made me laugh again. Agnes has hardly any *money.* But she has those little bits of stocks and she owns a house built in the 1750s and a half-acre lot on one of the nicest streets in town. Even allowing for its condition, I don't suppose you could buy that place for less than eighty thousand, and then there's the furniture. Nothing fabulously valuable, but some nice Victorian and Edwardian things—very popular these days. And if Agnes were in the nursing home, she'd *have* to sell it all to pay them, make no mistake. Oh, yes, I think there could be a profit motive in this. But don't go saying it around town. Some people wouldn't care for that at all."

I kissed her when I left, and she looked pleased, but warned, "Remember, what I've said doesn't necessarily mean Regis Warnke is wrong about Agnes. Perhaps she *can't* manage alone anymore."

"Don't worry," I said, "I'll remember. I'm also remembering what happened to a certain turtle. And believe me, *it isn't going to happen to Aunt Aggie.*"

CHAPTER 20

THERE were two messages for me at home. One had been stuck in the kitchen door. It was on a pink hospital slip and said, "Jo—Call Mrs. Pandakis tomorrow at the Governor's Office for Senior Citizens in F'burg after 1 pm. 555-4000 X 14. Say I sent you. Clara Parker." The other one Dad gave me. "There's some woman who says she's from the Board of Health who's been trying to get you for the last hour. Her number's on the pad there."

I sighed, remembering how I still didn't like telephones. This time the voice that answered was slightly affected, but the attitude was uncompromising. "I understahnd you've been acting as caretaker for Mrs. Pease." She made it sound as if I reported for work every morning with my mop and bucket. "I am the chairpehson of the Vicinity Board of Health, and a neighbor has complained about the prohperty. We would like to make an inspehction tomorrow at nine. Could you please be there with the keys?"

Ever since I had talked to Mrs. Lisle, I had been thinking hard and getting angrier. Mr. Follett, Dr. Warnke, and now this. I said as nicely as I could, "Oh, I'm afraid I couldn't do that. I'll be in school."

"Oh, you will?" She sounded surprised that I wouldn't skip school for her convenience. "Well in thaht case, three o'clock would do."

"I'm afraid I can't do that, either. I can't let anyone in the house without permission."

Advocacy: the presentation of another person's point of view, even when it isn't your own.

"Then you can telephone her."

"What a shame. That's impossible. She's in the hospital and has no phone. However," I added before she could interrupt, "I will be seeing Mrs. Pease about five o'clock tomorrow and I'll be glad to ask her then."

She gave up. "Very well. I'll expehct to hear from you tomorrow evening." She gave me her name and number and hung up.

I had bought some time, but not a lot. I figured this was an emergency. "Mother! Dad! I need you!"

"So, you see," I summarized a few minutes later, "if they go in there, they're going to find eight cat coffins in the cellar and three dead cats in a bureau.

Aunt Aggie will never agree to let them in, I know that. But what if they come with a policeman or something?"

"But *darling*!" said my mother. I had known she'd be horrified by the coffins. She went to a convent school where cleanliness was not just next to godliness but pushing it for first place.

"If they come with a policeman," said Dad, "it's out of your hands, isn't it? In fact, if you are really viewing yourself as Mrs. Pease's agent, or advocate, then it's out of your hands anyway. If she says no, it's no until they get a warrant or a court order, or whatever it takes."

"But Hal, *dead animals*!"

"I know. I agree. It sounds grim. But Jo has put herself in a special position here. She does what Mrs. Pease wants until the law tells her otherwise. And if the house is riddled with germs or something, the Board can deal with it."

And that, in the end, was the way we left it, at least until the next morning at eight o'clock. I was just on my way out the door with my books when the phone rang and an unfamiliar man's voice said, low and husky, "You the little gel that's mindin' Aggie Pease's place?"

I said yes.

"You don't know me," said the voice. "I live up Oak Street. Now, it may be none o' my business, an' it may not. Theyuh's a pahty of folks just goin' 'round through Aggie's side yahd. Guess they've gone in the house now, through the back. Aggie wouldn't like that much."

"No," I agreed, "she certainly wouldn't."

So in the end I did miss school on account of the Board of Health. I found them inside the house, three of them, clumping up and down the stairs, with cats escaping from the kitchen every which way. There was no need to ask which was the one I had talked to. It wasn't the round pink man with the face like bubble gum or the timid little woman who stood looking uncomfortable by the back door. Mrs. Laurance Stropner stood at the top of the stairs, and her expression was as iron-gray as her hair.

"Excuse me," I said, "I don't remember having given you Mrs. Pease's permission to enter her house. Or do you have a"—I was trying to remember the words Dad had used last night— "a court order or a warrant?"

"That won't be necessary," she said. "We found other means of getting in."

I had been hearing sounds from the animal room, and suddenly I knew what she meant. I went tearing around through the screen door and found Billy sitting in the rocker, squeezing Dolly almost to death and snuffling as he rocked. He looked just the way he had the day Mummy died. "Don't cry, Billy," I said. "Please don't cry. I know you couldn't help giving them your key."

"Aunt Aggie be mad. She be real mad."

"Don't worry, Billy, we'll get them to give it back

soon." There were two shiny tracks from his nose down to his chin. I got him some paper towels. Mrs. Stropner came down the stairs and I met her in the hall. I said, "Did you find any health hazards, or were you evaluating the furniture?" I knew the little dressing room was locked.

"Really, I don't know what you mean."

"Good. I certainly hope not."

"Hey, Selma!" called the pink man from the direction of the kitchen. "Come down in the cellar." I went down after them with my hands clenched tight and found him shining a flashlight into dark corners. "There's rats, all right," he said, pointing. The others nodded, although I couldn't see anything much. The man swung his light around and it caught on the pale sides of the coffins. "What's she doing, storing food down here?" He went over and looked at the coffins more closely. "Geez. Crosses! Excuse me, ladies." He pointed the light at me. "You mind telling us what's in there?"

"Dead cats."

"Ho-ly . . . !"

I had thought long and hard last night about what I would do when the Board got into the house. If I didn't answer when asked, they would open the boxes, and I thought Fluffy, Bonnie, and the others deserved their privacy. But when it came down to it, I didn't want anybody's health endangered, either, if that was what was happening.

The man and Mrs. Stropner had crowded around

the boxes. The other woman had retreated up the stairs, whimpering something about fresh air. The pink man picked up one of the coffins and looked at it closely. "Not bad work, you know. Airtight."

"I hope Billy Goodson appreciates the compliment," I said. "You scared him to death."

The pink man looked embarrassed. "Aw, c'mon, we didn't really do anything."

"Of course not. That's why he was crying." They went up the stairs ahead of me in an iron-gray silence. "By the way," I said, "I think Mrs. Pease has a right to know what your report is going to say."

The pink man smiled at me. He didn't like thinking of himself as the sort of person who would bully a retarded kid. "Oh, I don't think we got too big a problem here. There's rats in the cellar, but nothing an exterminator couldn't take care of. That's up to her, though. We just recommend. As to the other, there's no contamination of the water table that I can see. Wonderful how they built these old privies—"

"Now just a minute, Harry!" I didn't have to turn around to know who was talking. "I'm not at all sure I concur in thaht. This case should be disposed of in a rehgular meeting. There are issues here—"

Still squabbling, they started out the back door. "Excuse me," I said politely but loudly, "I'd like the key back." As I had suspected, it was Mrs. Stropner who had it. She took it out of her pocket but hesitated before giving it to me.

"I don't know," she said to the others, "I just don't think it's right to leave this place in charge of a—a teenager and a half-wit. Perhaps we should give this to the police."

I was beginning, just a little bit, to enjoy myself. "Oh, please do," I said. "It would save me the trouble of explaining to them how you got into Mrs. Pease's house without permission, through intimidating a person who can't defend himself."

At my mention of going to the police, the short woman began to whimper again. "Oh, dear. Selma. Harry. I said I was against this. I did."

Mrs. Stropner, of course, was tougher. She gave me a look of honest dislike as she handed over the key. " 'Can't defend himself,' eh? Well, that cehtainly doesn't apply to you. I suppose you're hanging around looking to be mentioned in her will. By the way, how did you know we were here?"

Triumph warmed me, but I kept it hidden. "How did I know? Why, in the same way, *exactly the same way,* you knew Billy would be there with the key at eight o'clock." Watching their faces, I knew that I'd guessed right.

After they left, it took Billy and me forty-five minutes to round up the cats that had filtered all over the house as soon as the screen door was open. The last one was little Pooky, who had somehow got into the attic and was so zonked on catnip she could hardly purr. I took a big bunch down for the others, and its lemony musky smell made one more ingredient in the familiar mix of camphor, cat, coal smoke, and privy.

When I finally got to school, I went to the office to explain why I was late. The secretary knew all about my involvement with Aunt Aggie by now. "There was an emergency at Mrs. Pease's," I told her.

"What sort of emergency?"

"Attempted burglary. They managed to get in, but nothing was taken except someone's privacy."

"It was Dr. Warnke," I said that night to my parents. "Mrs. Lisle told me he and somebody called Elmer Robb own the nursing home together. I'll bet Mr. Follett is a pal of theirs too. And the 'neighbor' who complained was the old lady next door, I'll bet you anything. You know who that is."

"Elmer's aunt, of course." Dad was making pizza crust, flipping the dough around on his fists like a revolving white circus tent.

"Right. Probably he got her to make the complaint, and then when I wouldn't let them in right away, they found out from Dr. Warnke about Billy's having a key. He's the only person I've ever told, and you know how secretive Aunt Aggie is."

"It could have been Mrs. Robb, though," objected Mother, looking up from simmering tomato sauce. "After all, she lives right next door."

"It could have, but I don't think so. Did you ever notice the size of that fence she's put up between their two houses? It's at least eight feet high and there isn't so much as a knothole to look through. I don't suppose it matters, though. Even if he didn't tell them about Billy, he had a darned good reason for setting the Board of Health on us." I finished putting out plates and sat down to slice mushrooms.

"Jo," said Dad, "you don't really believe Mrs. Stropner was trying to get the house condemned, do you? I think that's going too far. It could get the Board in all sorts of trouble, filing false reports and so on."

To my surprise, Mother came to my support. "Hal, you'd be absolutely amazed at what goes on in these nursing homes sometimes, financially, I mean. The accounting is so complicated, it's easy to hide all sorts of things like fraudulent Medicare payments, patients being billed for nonexistent treatment or facilities. Besides, they didn't really have to condemn the property. All they needed was to give Jo one more reason to think Mrs. Pease would be better off somewhere else. If it hadn't been for Mrs. Lisle, she'd probably have agreed."

That was the sore spot. I looked down at my mushrooms, seeing the beautiful way the caps curl under at the edges and the elegant pale brown color, like a Siamese cat's. "You know, I still wonder about that talk he had with me. He was so—so *nice,* and kind and concerned. Even Boots liked him. He made me feel good—that he trusted me to do the right thing and all. I guess I'm saying he flattered me, and I liked it. Boy, do I feel dumb."

Dad had the dough patted out into two big circles by now. His hands were sticky, but he came over and pulled my head up against him with the inside of his arm. "Honey, let me tell you something. Shakespeare knew all about your problem three hundred years ago. Remember Iago, who could 'smile, and smile, and be a villain'? At least you're not as badly off as poor Othello." I always know Dad's feeling good when he quotes Shakespeare, and of course he was right: nobody had been murdered.

As usual, Mother brought the conversation back to something practical. "So what are you going to do, Jo? I don't see how Mrs. Pease can go back to Sunnydale now, but what else is there?"

I remembered the poster I saw every time I went to Mrs. Parker's office. " 'Pray for the dead,' I guess, 'and fight like hell for the living.' Sorry, Mom, that's a quotation."

CHAPTER 21

LUCKILY, it was Saturday the next day, or I might have had to skip school again. I biked to the hospital and was in Aunt Aggie's room by nine o'clock. She was out of bed using her walker. It's like a little piece of aluminum fence that you can lean on when you walk. Aunt Aggie was slow with it, but she was getting around, and the nurse beside her was just holding her elbow lightly.

"I got to get all the practice I can," Aunt Aggie explained when she was in her chair again and the nurse had gone. "They're sendin' me back to *that place* this aftanoon, and I'll slip back, I just know I will."

"This afternoon? Listen, Aunt Aggie, I don't think you ought to go back there."

I looked to see whether she was startled, but her expression only seemed to say that at last I had come to my senses. "Aunt Aggie, some things have been happening; I don't have time to tell you. But your doctor, Dr. Warnke? You were right, he doesn't want you to go back to your house. He—he told me I should think about finding homes for the animals." I had said that last on purpose to make her mad, and I was delighted to see the old fire in her eye.

"That man's a fool," she declared. "I always said so. *Funny*dale, that's what they ought to call that place. But what a' we goin' to do?"

"You stay right there. I'm going to see Mrs. Parker. If they come for you with that ambulance, do something. I don't know what, but can you think of something?"

She gave me a scornful look. "Don't you worry. I'll have a dizzy spell."

As I hurried toward Mrs. Parker's office, I found myself passing Mrs. Lisle's room. Before I could think about it, I had gone in.

Mrs. Lisle put down her copy of *Menfreya in the Morning* by Victoria Holt, and by the time I finished telling her the problem, I almost had my breath back. Mrs. Lisle was frowning in a way that made me remember she had been a teacher. "It's very simple, dear. What Agnes needs now is another doctor."

"I thought she needed another nursing home."

"Yes, dear. But one can't just knock on the door and say, let me in. Fortunately, I think I can help. Hand me my phone, would you?" In the hospital, I now knew, bedside phones cost extra. Unlike Aunt Aggie, Mrs. Lisle had one. She had a brief conversation with someone named Jimmy, and hung up smiling. "My doctor," she explained. "Such a nice boy, he went to Harvard. I think he'll do very well for Agnes. Not that Agnes likes any doctor, I must warn him about that. Of course, he doesn't usually work on a Saturday, but I told him this was more important than planting peas so he's coming right over. It's very nice when people do just what you tell them to, but you have to form the habit early. I had Jimmy in the fourth grade."

"Mrs. Lisle," I said, "I think you're a good fairy, with a wand and everything."

Aunt Aggie went to the Mount Hope Nursing Home in West Parrington, not that Saturday but the following Monday. Dr. Jim Faulkner was young and thin, with freckled redhead's skin and a joking manner. He got along with Aunt Aggie by making it clear that all he wanted was to send her home. "We'll have you giving a dance recital in six months," he teased. "I'll be selling the tickets myself." About her reasons for leaving Sunnydale, he didn't want to hear. "That's all past history. I'm interested in the patient *now.* If she's lost confidence in her previous treatment, that's all I need to know."

Aunt Aggie didn't actually like Mount Hope. It was just as noisy as Sunnydale, and the food was only somewhat better. However, she did get to exercise more. When I biked out to see her—it was only about two miles farther than the hospital, though in another direction—she was almost always hitching up and down the corridors with the walker. Another good thing was that Mount Hope had a cat, a sleek silver tabby named Melville. Aunt Aggie wooed him with pouches of moist cat food and he soon took to spending most of his nap time on the foot of her bed. Also, one day during Easter vacation, I brought Dolly out to see her, yowling in a cardboard carrier.

Nothing happened as a result of the Board of Health's visit to Aunt Aggie's house, except that she got a letter recommending in very polite terms that she might wish to call an exterminator. I was surprised at how easily she agreed. Rats, it seemed, were not on her list of "poor little animals."

Mrs. Parker was thoughtful when I called her to explain what had happened. "Kiddo," she said, "it's not easy in this world to tell the sheep from the goats. Us nurses are so used to the idea that doctors are always right, sometimes I think we don't use our own heads enough. Those pills he was giving Aggie, now. Mostly tranquilizers and sleeping pills. Nothing you wouldn't give somebody who was very agitated—you know, upset, hysterical. And certainly well within the proper dosages. But did she really need that stuff? If you hadn't been around, nobody would even have asked. By the way, did you talk to Mrs. Pandakis?"

"Mrs. Who?" I had forgotten all about the note Mrs. Parker had left me.

When I finally did call, I got the first piece of good news Aunt Aggie had had in a long time. There was something called the Anna Emmeline Benson Trust that paid money to "unmarried ladies of Vicinity, Massachusetts, over seventy years of age." Anna Emmeline had been a suffragist who once chained herself to President McKinley's front door. She died about 1910. I promised myself I would read more about her someday, and Mother Jones too. I wondered whether Anna Emmeline had lived in the Benson House, and pictured her as an old lady waving to little Agnes in her white pinafore. There was a thread there, weaving in and out of the big quilt that was Vicinity. I didn't want to lose it.

The trust wouldn't pay Aunt Aggie much, just four hundred a month, but that would cover one thing: She could hire someone to come in and "do" for her a few hours every day. The arthritis was as much a problem as the hip, and unlike the hip, it wouldn't improve with time. Mother brought the papers concerning the trust home with her from Frontburg, and another set about state fuel assistance for the elderly. I was getting pretty good at filling things out by now.

Then Dr. Faulkner announced that he would send

Aunt Aggie home on the tenth of May if she kept up the good work with the walker. I was there when he told her, and she cried, surprising us all three. "I nevuh thought I'd see this day," she sobbed.

"But Aunt Aggie, you always said you'd get home to your babies."

"Don't be foolish, Joan. What people say an' what they think ain't always the same." Actually, it was a lesson I'd thought I'd already learned, but I went back and studied it again. Aunt Aggie had a way of keeping you humble.

It was less than two weeks before Aunt Aggie was due home, and I began to be even busier than before. I had long ago decided that the place had to get a good cleaning before she came back, but she was insistent that nothing should be moved. "You can tidy the kitchen," she agreed, "but leave things out so's I can find 'em."

When I mentioned the cleaning to Jenny, she instantly turned it into a project. "You can't do all that by yourself, Johanna Justine, it's too yucky. What you want is to organize it, get people to volunteer, and make it fun."

I was not used to thinking of hordes of people as fun, but Jenny was right. We put up a notice in the high school, with a cat cartoon by Elizabeth and lettering by Dan, and soon we had commitments for the Saturday before the tenth of May from six kids and Jenny's older brother Jay, who was studying at Lowell Tech.

Jay was really a help, because he had a custodian's job at the college. He arranged to borrow one of the powerful industrial vacuum cleaners he worked with, and he bought us five gallons of industrial cleaning liquid. "Wear gloves when you use it," he warned us. "It'll take the paint off a truck or the hide off a bear, but germs don't like it a bit."

On the Saturday, I got to the house early and took the cats, all twelve, up to the bedrooms. Little Annie scampered joyfully out into the backyard for the day. She had gotten thinner since Dr. Finnegan suggested I put her on a diet, and she looked more like a spaniel now and less like a pillow with four legs. Then I began throwing open all the windows, and before I was finished the crew arrived, looking scraggly because we were all wearing clothes we could afford to throw away. We were going to scrub down only the animal room, kitchen, and pantry. The parlor and dining room would be dusted and vacuumed. It was a yucky job, as Jenny had said, and I was amazed and grateful at the way she, Dan, Jason, Elizabeth, Jay, Jason's friend Phil, and a stubby girl from across the street named Sarah Bent waded right in and did it. And Jenny was right: it was fun—or almost.

Some of the work was rough going. We had to wear the face masks Jay had brought because of the dust, which he said could give you lung disease, and the details of what was under the sink and behind the cabinets were just as bad as I'd thought they'd be. We took the old refrigerator outside and scrubbed every inch of it, and we scraped and scrubbed every single thing in the kitchen, helped out by the music from Jason's radio. Sarah took all the bedclothes over to her house to be washed and aired, and we were all surprised to discover that the woodwork in the animal room was not gray but a nice light green.

About midmorning, people started coming by with offerings or advice or just to stare, and we learned that yesterday's *Vicinity Voice* had had an article headed LOCAL TEENS RALLY ROUND. One woman brought a case of cat food she said she'd had since her cat died. A man in a truck brought ten twenty-pound bags of coal and wouldn't tell me his name. "Just say it's for Shep," he said. "She'll know." Then, around noon, a van pulled up by Aunt Aggie's stone gateposts. To our surprise, out got Mr. Koumenis, who runs Vicinity's only pizza place. He handed us three whole pizzas—one pepperoni, one mushroom, one meatball, all with extra cheese. "It's a nice t'ing you kids're doing, a nice t'ing. I read it in the papers. You eat good, you hear?" We cheered him loudly because lunch was something we'd all forgotten to bring. We took the pizzas over to Sarah's clean green lawn to eat.

When we got through with the floors and the woodwork in the animal room, we started on the walls. "We'll have to take the wallpaper down," I said. "If we dust it, it'll just fall off." We began pulling at the saggy old paper, which hung in dangles like Mr. Follett's jowls. It came off in a shower of cobwebs and dust.

"Blast," said Jay, "we'll have to vacuum again." But even when we had done that, the walls looked horribly bare, with brownish cracks and pits in them.

"You know something?" I said slowly. "The bathroom upstairs is *full* of wallpaper."

"Wallpaper?"

"Uh-huh. Mrs. Pease's husband worked for a wallpaper company. It must be awfully old, though." We all went up to the bathroom to see.

"This is sort of pretty," said Sarah. "At least it's cheerful." Among the rolls of gray and maroon stripes, faded blue tulips, and dreary patterns of tan squares, we'd found three rolls of green lattices and climbing pink roses on a cream background.

"I'll have to ask her," I warned. "Maybe she doesn't want new paper."

But Jenny was already in love with it. "Just tell her it's the same green as the woodwork. It really is, see?"

"There isn't enough time left to do it this afternoon, and besides, we have to use the flea bombs."

"I'll come back tomorrow."

"So will I."

"Me too, right after church."

We finished the walls at four o'clock the next afternoon, exhausted, sticky, and hilarious. I had never put up wallpaper before, but Phil and Elizabeth both had. "Are you sure it's okay? The place in the corner where it's upside down?" Dan was a perfectionist.

"It's gorgeous," I said. "And besides, Aunt Aggie would need her glasses to notice. She never wears her glasses." We were all standing outside admiring the way the newly washed downstairs windows shone. A man came down the sidewalk with a basset hound on a leash. "So you're the kids cleaning out this dump," he said. "I hate to see you wasting your time."

"How come?" asked Dan neutrally.

"I know her," said the man. "Way back. Twenty, thirty years. Take it from me, she doesn't need your help. Aggie could buy and sell us all." He grinned significantly and jerked his head toward the house. "Loaded," he said. "Better off in that nursing home anyway." He went on up the street with a satisfied smile.

"What a jerk," said Jason. "Imagine anybody living that way who didn't have to."

It was just at that moment that Dr. Finnegan arrived, in a red-and-white van with bubble windows. He got out and came around to me. For some reason, he seemed embarrassed. "Johanna? I came because, well, I thought it would be nice if I wormed the cats and gave them their shots."

"Buy why? It's very nice of you, but why?"

He sat down on the step of his van with his knees

apart and ran his clasped hands through his hair. "You kids promise you'll never, never tell?"

Naturally, we all said yes.

"Well," he said, half laughing, half horrified, "I've gone and lost the corpse."

"You mean *the corpse*?" I asked. Suddenly it was terribly funny. "He's lost a dead cat of Aunt Aggie's," I explained. "She likes to get them back."

"You're kidding, man," said Phil. "How do you lose a dead cat?"

Dr. Finnegan straightened up and tried to look serious. "To be specific, I didn't lose it, my assistant did. There are service companies for vets that cart away dead animals and dispose of them sanitarily. Barry gave them the wrong freezer bag, that's all, and I just don't know what I'll tell Agnes."

There was a silence broken by giggles while we considered his dilemma.

"Power failure," said Jason. "It's the only way."

"Hunh?"

"You've got to tell her you had a power failure. You know, like when there's a hurricane and the hamburger spoils."

"Jason! Gross!"

"Of course," Jason went on, thinking out loud, "you'll have to say you buried it somewhere else, like under your favorite rosebush. That ought to be all right."

"Brilliant," said Dr. Finnegan. "By gosh, that's brilliant. I'll do it. Uh . . . I don't suppose you'd like to tell her for me? No, I didn't think so. But it's a great idea. Really."

We all took Dr. Finnegan upstairs and helped him dose the cats. "They're looking fine," he said. "You took good care of them. And Annie's not so obese, either. If I could just stop Mrs. Pease from hanging camphor around their necks when they have colds."

"Oh? Is that bad?" I asked.

"It's not good. It irritates the sinuses, but I can't convince her of that."

"Of course not," I said. "Aunt Aggie doesn't believe in being convinced of things."

CHAPTER 22

ANOTHER thing that happened in those days before Aunt Aggie came home was my little chat with Mr. Stropner. The rest of the group had been busy for some time getting kids to sign a petition for a literary magazine, and by now they had quite a few names, from all classes.

When the petition was about as long as we thought it would get, Jenny and Jason took it to Mr. S. and were turned down in less than ten seconds. "Boom!" said Jason. "Just like that. 'The situation hasn't changed.' "

Nobody noticed when I went off with the discarded petition.

I had it folded in the pocket of my jacket when I had my own appointment with Mr. Stropner the next day. The statewide English competency exams were only about two weeks away. I began on that subject. "I've been worrying a lot about the comps, Mr. Stropner. Everybody takes them very seriously around here because of the way you've put this school up at the top statewide."

He was not a mean man. In fact, part of his success came from giving confidence to the nervous.

He said, "Now, now, Jo, I don't think you need to worry too much. Your work has improved a great deal since this fall." (The truth was, by being as dull as I possibly could, I had squeezed an A minus out of him for an essay on "Massachusetts: Cranberry Capital of the Nation.")

"Oh," I said, trying to look as wide-eyed as possible, "but it's not *my* scores I'm worried about, it's some of these other people: Dan Neff, Harmony Wales, Pat Rao, Lucinda Cray, Karl De Niro—" I stopped when I saw I had his attention. Every one of the people I had mentioned had had outstanding scores in the comps last year; Karl De Niro, a junior, had had the highest score in the school. "It would be awful if they were distracted from studying, just at the most crucial time, but I'm afraid that's just what might happen. You see, a lot of people are sort of disappointed about the literary magazine." He wasn't stupid, either, at least not that way.

"Jo Morse, I can see just what you're up to, and that play isn't going to score. I don't know what made you think intimidation would work with me."

He started getting red, up inside the points of the M at his hairline.

"Now, isn't it funny you should say that? I've been studying up on intimidation recently. You know—getting a little practical experience. I've been observing the methods of the Board of Health. They intimidated a retarded kid very successfully, at the same time as other people were trying to intimidate an old woman and a teenager. In fact, I've found my experiences so enlightening that I'm trying to interest a small group in publishing a newsletter on local government. Under the History department, of course.

"On the other hand." I looked at him hard to make sure he was still paying attention. "On the other hand, I know I'd never have time for a newsletter if I were busy with a literary magazine. And I know a lot of students who would probably want to improve their writing if they had a magazine to work on: parallel structure, agreement, comma splices, and all that. They'd push other people too. You're so right about things being a team effort. You see, we're really counting on making you part of our magazine team, and I just know you're going to say yes. I just know it."

I was wrong about that, however. He didn't say anything, not a single word, as he signed my permission form.

"But how—?" began Lucinda.

"But what—?" sputtered Jason when I'd found the group and told them. "How did you know it would work, J.J.? He could have thrown you out of his office."

"I didn't really know it would work," I admitted. "Not a hundred percent. But it seemed like something worth fighting for—fighting like hell for," I added. "Besides, you haven't met *Mrs.* Stropner, and I have. He's had practice at being intimidated, believe me."

So, at last, Aunt Aggie came home to the house on Oak Street, to be greeted ecstatically by Annie, Midnight, Mittens, Goldie, Whitey, Daisy, Dolly, Dottie, Niggy, Willie, Pooky, Cuddles, and Fiddle. The house smelled different now, with the scent of lilacs blowing through open windows, but I didn't delude myself that it would stay that way, and as if to prove my point, Annie got so excited, she made a puddle on the floor.

Boots was delighted and astonished a few days later when I showed him his Aunt Aggie back at home, and thrilled when she handed him a fuzzy blue stuffed kitty with a bell around its neck. "Somebody gave me that in the nuhsin' home," she said. "Thought I was a baby, I guess. I been savin' it fuh my little angel Bobby."

"I'm not a angel," said Boots firmly. "They wear

dresses." He was growing toward four, and wanting everybody to know it.

I had much less work to do for Aunt Aggie now, which was a relief. The housekeeper did the shopping and cleaning, but as I had expected, getting a housekeeper was a problem. Aunt Aggie started out with a girl who had been an aide at Mount Hope and wanted a part-time job closer to home. She was pleasant and sweet, and lasted about three days. "That gel couldn't do an'thin'," said Aunt Aggie. "Couldn't cook, couldn't sew, couldn't drink a cup of tea 'less you told huh how." That was Terry. Then came Mary, who was middle-aged and talked too much, and Carrie, who was in her sixties and did all right until Aunt Aggie found out (or decided) she drank. After Terry, Mary, and Carrie, I lost track and was never really sure whether it would be Cherry, Gerry, or Sheri who would greet me at the door.

I went right on keeping the checkbook, and never did anything about the trouble at the bank. Dad had had a chat about it with a lawyer who often came into the store. (She read political thrillers.) "As long as Mrs. Pease acknowledges it as her signature and you don't use it for fraudulent purposes," Dad told me, "the bank can't do a thing about it. Kate also says she'd be delighted to lodge a complaint with the Board of Health or sue them for unauthorized entry, whichever Mrs. Pease prefers."

"Well, please don't mention it to Aunt Aggie. She

might want to do it, and I like things peaceful, just the way they are."

It was truly a wonderful spring, though the weather, as usual, switched from hot to cold and back without ever going through balmy. I think I thought that spring would go on forever, simply because it felt so good. My Cassandra self had gone into hiding, or I would have known better.

Watermelon had acquired a friend, a little white Persian cat. She would come by our house and the two of them would sit and wail at each other for hours through the window screen. If we came and caught them at it, Watermelon would look embarrassed and stalk off. "Why, you dirty old man," said Dad. "She's a third your age, and besides, you're only a consultant."

The really warm weather of June came, and we began to worry that we might have to shut all the downstairs windows at night to keep the two of them from yowling love songs at each other. "Does that cat live around here?" asked Mother. "I wish her owners would keep her in."

"I think she belongs to the people who rented the top floor at the Hansens'," I said. "I saw her once on their upstairs porch."

Then one day, when I arrived at Aunt Aggie's to write some checks, she greeted me with an air of mystery. "Wait till you see what I got in my spayuh room," she said, very pleased. "Go on up. It's the one on the right."

Inside the spare room was a young, fluffy white cat, with a cat box, a water dish, and a food dish all neatly lined up against the foot of a marble-topped bureau. She came right up to me to be rubbed. I noticed she had a flea collar on and her fur was as soft as a rabbit's, except that there was a bare, flaky patch of skin on her back. She had beautiful gold eyes, so dark they were almost bronze, the kind only real Persians have. I petted her all over, told her she was a gorgeous girl, and went back downstairs.

Aunt Aggie was sitting in the animal room with Fiddle on her lap. The blue housedress she wore was neatly darned now, thanks to one of the housekeepers, and I could smell potatoes boiling on the stove. "Ain't that little kitty a beauty, now? I'm goin' to call huh Snowball."

I sat down in the other chair, the little armless rocker with the splintery seat. It prickled through the back of my shorts. Something else was prickling also. It was like the time I had opened the upstairs bureau: I could feel the situation before I could see it. "Aunt Aggie, I have some really good news. I think I know who owns that cat."

"Well, if they do, they don't desuhve to. That cat's been *abused*."

"Abused? My goodness, she looks healthy to me. Someone's kept her brushed, or that long fur would be all full of mats and burrs."

"Brushed uh not, she's been *abused.* Didn't you see huh back?"

"Oh, that. But that's just summer eczema, isn't it? Watermelon gets it, too, sometimes."

"That ain't eczema, that's *abuse*." And from the way she said it, the subject was dismissed. We did checks and went through the mail, and I wrote a note for her to her medium friend Mitzi, thanking her for some candy. I was always interested in Mitzi because I still hadn't figured out exactly what it was that Aunt Aggie and she believed, to make Aunt Aggie keep dead cats in the house. Was it life after death, like the Egyptians—cats and people packed away in their pyramids with toys and food and clothes for the next world? Mummy the mummified cat? Or was it reincarnation, or the idea of lots of little furry souls hovering around the house? I had never told her I'd stumbled on that last secret, and I was sure the Board of Health would do everything they could to prevent her from finding out about their visit.

I addressed the note, stamped it and the bills, and said I would put them in our mailbox. It was time for supper, but I sat for a minute, seeing the shiny metal grin on the little parlor stove, the silvery purple chains of wisteria drooping down over the windows, the room warm and restless with cats. I had felt very good in that room, getting done what needed doing, seeing things working out. I got up and went over to the other chair, moving the walker out of the way so I could kiss her. I was glad to see she was wearing her pearl earrings. She had taken to dressing up more since she got home from the hospital, and the cigar boxes full of jewelry sat on top of the little trunk now, although the diamond and the star sapphire were safe in the bank. "Take care, Aunt Aggie," I said, putting the walker back where she could get it. "I'll mail these as soon as I get home."

I had even less time left than I thought. As soon as I walked into the kitchen, Mother said, "By the way, have you seen that white cat recently? A young man named Beardsley came by asking for it. They're worried about it because it needs to take medicine."

"Yes. I know where it is, actually. Did Mr. Beardsley leave a number?"

"Here it is. What's the matter, Johanna?"

"I need to use the phone, is all. Can I tell you later?"

I went upstairs and took the hall phone with its long cord around the corner into my bedroom. I was afraid I might change my mind if I waited. "Aunt Aggie, it's Johanna. Remember those people I said had a white Persian cat? Their name is Beardsley and they've been looking everywhere for her. They need to give her medicine for her eczema. Don't you think you ought to tell them you've found her?"

"I ain't tellin' anybody nothin'. That cat's abused, don't you unduhstand?"

"Aunt Aggie." I could feel my throat closing up. "If that were your cat, wouldn't you feel just awful if someone found it and kept it? They'll think it's been run over or hurt."

"Now, don't you worry 'bout *them,* Joan. Anybody who'd do that to a cat has just got no feelin's."

Unseen by her, I pressed my fist to my mouth, then took it away again. "Aunt Aggie. That cat is theirs. I can't lie to them. I'll have to tell them where I've seen it."

"You do, and you'll nevuh entuh this house again. A puhson that tol-rates animal abuse ain't welcome heyuh."

"I know, Aunt Aggie. I'm sorry. But I have to do it." I wiped some tears off my face and called the Beardsleys before I could change my mind.

For quite a while after that, I felt angry and hurt at the way Aunt Aggie had treated me. Jenny and Jason and the rest were even more indignant than I was. At the same time, we were all fascinated by the news bulletins we soon began getting from Sarah Bent. "There was a man at her house last night, banging and calling, but she wouldn't let him in," she told us first, and the next day, "They came back with a police officer, Charlie Savineau. He started out nice and polite, but they all ended up shouting. Mrs. Pease was leaning out of the window and giving it to them, and you could hear her all the way to Main Street." In spite of myself, I had to smile. Aunt Aggie must have enjoyed that.

The last item came two days later. "They got the cat, but it took the two of them and two policemen.

They threatened to take her down to the station and she shook her fist at them out the window and yelled that she was a poor old invalid with no one to help her, and she called Chief Amory a hooligan and a highway robber and a vivisector before they were out of there and Mrs. Robb next door came out on her porch in her nightgown and told Mrs. Pease to shut up. I don't even know what a vivisector is."

"Take it from me," I said. "In Aunt Aggie's book, it's the worst word there is."

I missed Aunt Aggie a lot, but I never went to her house again, though she did call me on the phone one evening. A hoarse and unmistakable voice said in my ear when I answered, "Troublemakuh! That's all you ah, a troublemakuh! I knew it when I fust seen you. The sufferin' of that cat is youh fault, an' I hope you know it."

"Aunt Aggie, I'm sorry you feel like that. I hope you'll change your mind someday." My answer was the crash of the phone hanging up.

Mother thought she'd forget all about it after a while, but Dad shook his head. "She hasn't spoken to Bea Langley in—how long? Ten years? I think Jo's right. She won't change her mind."

In September, Mrs. Lisle was in the hospital again, "for observation," and as I was riding up to see her in the elevator one day, Dr. Warnke stepped in. "Why, it's Johanna Morse," he said with a sad shake of his head. "I was very disappointed in you, Johanna. Perhaps now you regret your hardheadedness. I heard about that cat Mrs. Pease was stealing. A typical senile episode. And now she's cut you off and is putting it all around town how you took advantage of her. Johanna, I don't understand you."

It was hard, even then, to be around him without wanting to agree with him. He sounded so concerned, so reasonable. At the same time, however, something began echoing in my head: *hardheaded, hard-shelled, hardheaded, hard-shelled.* A wrinkled old fighter, trapped in a garbage can. Caged or free, the snapping turtle still snaps.

"I'm sorry," I said. "It's a very long story. About fourteen cats and a dead turtle. And somebody called Mother Jones. I don't think you'd understand." As I got out and went down the hall, I thought I could stop being mad at Aunt Aggie; I still had the living to fight for.

The person most affected by the news that Aunt Aggie wasn't speaking to me was Boots. I wished he had cried or complained but instead he accepted the fact so easily, and so knowingly. The look in his eyes told me that Aunt Aggie had merely joined the parade of people who didn't have time for a little boy with a big name. When he began collecting toads and worms and bugs in jars, I let him keep them at my house, even though I disliked the idea almost as much as his mother. Our reasons were different, though: She hated the creatures; I hated the cages.

Mother's birthday came and Dad took her dancing in Boston. But though she wore her favorite blue silk dress, there was no star sapphire ring. I had learned some things that year, so I didn't ask Dad about the ring until we were alone.

"You're right," he said. "She sold it last spring when the loan ran out. You weren't supposed to know about it. It was just enough to take us through until things got better. I was about ready to chuck it and start pumping gas."

Then for just a minute I pictured another star sapphire ring, with a tag on it saying, "This is to go to Joan Morse, my most faithful friend," and later glowing on my mother's hand as she danced in blue silk under the stars. "From J.J. with love." Had I, after all, been too hardheaded, as Dr. Warnke had called it? Was a Persian cat really worth it? But that was silly, of course. The cat had nothing to do with it. It was Aunt Aggie herself who had taught me to be hardheaded.

Over a year later, we heard that Dr. Warnke was in court for tax evasion. Mother was especially pleased. "You see? It was the bookkeepers that got him in the end."

That was also the year Mrs. Lisle died, suddenly, in her sleep.

* * *

Mrs. Pease still lives on Oak Street. One time not so long ago, a group of townspeople got together and decided they'd paint her house for her. They got painters and hardware stores to volunteer advice and materials, and were all set to put the green back on the shutters and the cream on the clapboards. It was only when she found out they would have to cut the wisteria down in order to paint behind it that she said no, thank you, she'd keep the house as it was. I was glad, in a way. I was afraid that the next time I went by they'd have rooted out the crazy, beautiful garden and made it look just like every other house in town.

About the Author

Georgess McHargue grew up in New York City and was graduated from Radcliffe College. She is a former editor of children's books but now devotes her time to writing; she is the author of more than twenty books. Ms. McHargue and her husband, archaeologist Michael Roberts, are the parents of one daughter, Mairi. They live in an eighteenth-century house in Groton, Massachusetts.